Leonor Park

Bilingual Press/Editorial Bilingüe

General Editor
    Gary D. Keller

Managing Editor
    Karen S. Van Hooft

Associate Editor
    Ann M. Waggoner

Assistant Editor
    Linda St. George Thurston

Editorial Consultants
    Julia C. Angelica
    Jennifer Hartfield Prochnow

Editorial Board
    Juan Goytisolo
    Francisco Jiménez
    Eduardo Rivera
    Severo Sarduy
    Mario Vargas Llosa

Address:
Bilingual Review/Press
Hispanic Research Center
Arizona State University
Tempe, Arizona 85287
(602) 965-3867

Leonor Park

Nash Candelaria

Bilingual Press/Editorial Bilingüe
TEMPE, ARIZONA

ISBN 0-927534-18-5
Printed simultaneously in a softcover edition. ISBN 0-927534-19-3

Library of Congress Cataloging-in-Publication Data

Candelaria, Nash.
    Leonor Park / by Nash Candelaria.
        p.   cm.
    ISBN 0-927534-18-5 (cloth) : $20.00. — ISBN 0-927534-19-3 (paper) : $12.00
    I. Title.
    PS3553.A4896L46   1991
    813'.54—dc20   91-20652
                                                             CIP

PRINTED IN THE UNITED STATES OF AMERICA

Cover design by Thomas Detrie

Back cover photo by Michael Collopy

Acknowledgments

This volume is supported by a grant from the Arizona Commission on the Arts, a State agency.

Song lyrics are excerpted from "Sunday" by Ned Miller, Chester Conn, Jule Styne, and Bennie Krueger, copyright © 1926 by Leo Feist, Inc., New York; "Collegiate" by Moe Jaffe and Nat Bonx, copyright © 1925 by Shapiro, Bernstein & Co., Inc., New York; "My Blue Heaven" by Walter Donaldson and George Whiting, copyright © 1927 by Leo Feist, Inc., New York; and "All Alone" by Irving Berlin, copyright © 1924 by Irving Berlin, Inc., New York.

This story owes a debt of gratitude to the works of two authors: Marc Simmons, Historian of the Santa Fe Trail and author of *Albuquerque, A Narrative History,* and Thorton Wilder, author of *Our Town,* the classic American play of small town life.

Part One

1

June 20, 1985

"Dear Papá,

"I will arrive Monday, the first, at two in the afternoon, flight 107, Continental Airlines. I hear they 'retired' your driver's license, so don't do anything foolish like picking me up. And don't send anyone. I plan to rent an air-conditioned car.

"A colleague is taking over my classes that week. The department chairman finally relented when I told him how important it was that I attend the 100th anniversary of incorporation of the city that my ancestors helped found. Frankly, you know how I *really* feel about it. But I am pleased to join you during the dedication of the land that Mother donated to the city for a park.

"I finally found part of that manuscript that you wanted to read. When the Centennial Committee turned down the play, I got madder than hell and tore it up. It wasn't so much that they turned it down, although that hurt. It was the reason they gave. That it was derivative and not an original piece of work. Which means that they were too illiterate to see the universality of Wilder's play and how beautifully it adapted to the celebration. Then they added in their snotty way: it really was too narrow in focus, not truly representing the breadth of the city's history and population. So I tore it up, every damned page of it. I should waste my creative efforts on their bigoted and ignorant ways.

"When you said you wanted to see it, I got angry all over again. This time from guilt. Luckily I had a draft of the first act, which I ran through the copy machine at the university and have enclosed. It should give you an idea. Acts II and III were better I think. Act II with its lovely scene of the young girl and boy finally discovering that they were in love. And act III where the dead talk to each other while watching the living suffer their insignificant soap operas.

"At any rate, I hope you enjoy reading act I. You may recognize it. A movie was made of the original play some years ago. And, of course, every college and high school in the country performs it every other season. It is, as the critics say, *the* classic American play of small town life.

"As for the damned committee's criticism that it is derivative, Wilder himself, referring to another of his plays, writes in the introduction to a published volume of his works: 'The play is deeply indebted to James Joyce's *Finnegan's Wake*. I should be very happy if, in the future, some author should feel similarly indebted to any work of mine.' Well, here it is. If only there were some theater people on the committee instead of all those real estate developers and lawyers. They might have shared Wilder's tolerance and dealt more kindly with this version. Instead, I hear, they're doing some piece of crap about Billy the Kid. Talk about narrow focus!

"But enough carping. I look forward to seeing you and the old town again. Your grandchildren send their love. What with school, work, and the insufficient funds that are the natural condition of young adults, they will be with us in spirit rather than body during the celebration.

"I'll see you Monday afternoon.

With love, your son,
Tony"

Antonio Rafa took off his thick-lensed glasses and wiped them with a wrinkled handkerchief. He peered through the lenses at the lighted bulb of the floor lamp, set his spectacles back in place, blew his nose, and stuffed his handkerchief in the hip pocket of his trousers.

His wrinkled face twitched in a smile. There was a time, years ago, when any such letter from his youngest son would have disturbed him. But now he could even put up with a week of Tony's restless presence and volatile emotions. It was no more than the buzzing of a summer fly, and at Antonio's age, nearly eighty, a fly was just another of God's creatures, entitled to its buzzing.

The old man stared at the letter again, remembering rather than rereading it, then laid it on the dining table which he used as his desk. He weighed the manuscript in his hand: it felt like half an hour if his eyes didn't tire too quickly. Then he began to read, feeling a thrill like seeing a grandbaby for the first time, a baby that he knew was beautiful no matter what anyone else said.

2

Nuestro pueblo

ACT I

The bare stage is dimly lit, the curtain open. As the audience settles, the Stage Manager enters. He wears a rancher's Stetson felt hat, jeans, and a blue workshirt with sleeves rolled above his elbows. Downstage right there is an unpainted table with two crude, unpainted benches, one on either side of it. Downstage left is a similar table with benches.

The Stage Manager surveys the stage slowly, then turns to face the audience as the house lights fade. When the theater is dark, he speaks with a barely perceptible accent—it is more a rhythm, a syncopation, than an accent—but it is enough to let the audience know that English is not his only language. Perhaps not even his primary language. When he pronounces a Spanish word, he does it correctly and unselfconsciously.

* * *

STAGE MANAGER: I'm going to take you on a tour of nuestro pueblo. The name of the settlement—it's not exactly a town. It's more a village. A few adobe houses clustered not too far from the plaza, and little adobe farmhouses north and upriver. It used to have a name in its own right until the railroad and the Anglos, the non-Hispanic peoples, came from back east and started New Town which took over. We call it Old Town. And the old-timers, those who remember when everybody around here spoke only Spanish, sometimes call it Los Rafas. Los Rafas, New Mexico, beside the Río Grande: latitude 35 degrees 5 minutes north;

longitude 106 degrees 38 minutes west. It's May 5, 1912. There's an early morning glow behind the Sandía Mountains on the east mesa. *(The stage lights slowly turn up.)* Sandía means watermelon in Spanish, and the mountains are shaped like a slice of watermelon. The sun is chasing the moon west toward Navajoland. *(He slowly walks upstage as the lights get brighter.)* Let's take a look around nuestro pueblo . . . Just past the plaza is Railroad Avenue which leads to New Town. Some of the civic minded want to change the name to Central Avenue. The railroad station is a mile-and-a-half east. Across the tracks, up on the heights, they'll eventually build new, big homes where the rich people will live. Right now the sanitariums are in the heights. The lungers from back east come here to take the cure for their tuberculosis. The altitude and the air make them well. *(Pointing upstage.)* San Felipe Church is on the north side of the plaza. It's been here over two hundred years . . . The Protestant churches are in New Town. The Congregational church was the first. Then the Methodist. The Episcopalian. Presbyterian. Baptist. Lutheran. Even an African Methodist Episcopal church for los negros. And the Jewish temple . . . The Anglos have more churches, but we have more people who attend. The county courthouse and jail are here in Old Town. We have one of the two post offices, a branch. Ours used to be the only one. But things seem to move to New Town after a while. The courthouse and jail will too one of these days. It's called progress . . . President Theodore Roosevelt visited here in 1903. He's very popular. He had been here before, recruiting Rough Riders for the Spanish-American War. Lots of our boys joined . . . Old Town has its own stores, but you can ride the electric trolley from the plaza to the big stores in New Town if you want. The Spanish-speaking people still shop in Old Town for the most part . . . The Old Town elementary school is over there. *(Points upstage right.)* You can hear the kids playing from the plaza. The high school is in New Town. *(He strolls to the table and benches stage right.)* This is Señor Lucero's house. People call him Doc even though he's not a real doctor. He's a veterinarian. A horse doctor. *(There are two trees behind the bench.)* That's a cottonwood tree. *(Points.)* And an apple. The house is adobe. The Luceros grow pinto beans, corn, chilis, tomatoes; not many flowers. These are practical people. They have to be. Like most, Doc

Lucero grows much of what his family eats. (*He crosses the stage.*)
Next door is Señor Baca's place. He works on the newspaper and
does a little farming on the side to make ends meet. (*He points
upstage.*) That's his field. Lots of corn. (*He looks out at the
audience.*) It's a nice pueblo . . . Nobody famous ever came from
here . . . The earliest markers in the church cemetery say 1706.
Armijos and Pereas. Luceros and Bacas. Names that are still
here . . . Old Town is dark except for the lights in a little adobe
house upriver. A young señora just had a baby boy there. And in
the church rectory, Father Martínez is meditating, getting ready
for early mass . . . In New Town paper boys and milkmen are at
work. Old man Ebert at the depot is waiting for the 5:30 bound
for Los Angeles. (*As the train whistle blows, the Stage Manager
takes out his pocketwatch.*) On the farms oil lamps have been lit for
a while. Country people have chores to do. Town people can
sleep late. Even Old Town people. Another day is yawning and
stretching and coming awake . . . Doc Lucero is walking slowly
down Railroad Avenue from what he thought was just a sick cow.
His wife is bustling about getting breakfast.

*Señora Lucero, a wiry, thin woman in her thirties, enters right. She
pushes open the shutters of her kitchen window and lights the fire in
her wood stove.*

*   *   *

Antonio read on. He could not remember the Old Town of 1912.
He had been but a boy of four then. How would his son, Tony, know
about those times? Yet it rang true.

He read about the meeting between Doc Lucero and the paper
boy. About the ordinary, everyday life. When the Stage Manager
watched the boy go off and told of what happened to him, Antonio
nodded. That was the way things happened.

"José had brains," he read. "He graduated first in his class in high
school. Won a scholarship to the university. He was first in his class
there too. José dreamed of becoming a teacher and helping his people.
His Model T crashed off Highway 66 on the way to California the
summer he graduated. He died in a hospital in Flagstaff, Arizona. Qué
lástima. How sad."

The woodcutter is driving his loaded wagon through the plaza. Another ordinary job on an ordinary day. How long had it been since Antonio had started a wood fire in an old wood stove?

Then, of course, the Lucero and Baca families. Their children. The slow, calm, innocent life that one always remembered from the past, even if it wasn't true. The veterinarian who delivered a baby son to the wife of the farmer whose cow was sick. The son who forgot to chop wood for his mother but remembered about his baseball game. The daughter, smartest in her high school class.

> *"The railroad shop whistle sounds in the distance. The children rush to the breakfast tables. On the right, Jorge Lucero, age fifteen, and María Lucero, age ten. On the left, Amelia and Guillermo Baca, about the same ages."*

Then the Stage Manager is looking at his pocketwatch and speaking: "We all set our clocks by the shop whistle. They repaired engines for the Santa Fe Railroad. The railroads got rich, and they brought a lot of jobs—to Old Town and New Town people both."

Breakfast and off to school. The same loving chidings of every mother to every child. Finally, their breakfast chores done, Señora Lucero and Señora Baca are chatting while one feeds the chickens and the other peels chilis. Señora Lucero is being offered a large sum of money for the old squash-blossom silver Indian necklace her mother left her. Money that, if she had it, she would use for a trip for her too-hard working husband and herself. A trip to New York or Chicago. "Before you die," Señora Lucero says, "you ought to see something—something big—and grand. Where they never heard of chili and beans and never will."

* * *

STAGE MANAGER: Muchas gracias, señoras. (*Señora Lucero and Señora Baca disappear into their homes.*) Now for some information about the town. A learned account. Professor Fergusson from the university has volunteered to give a few facts about our history. Professor Fergusson. (*Professor Fergusson, dressed in western suit, boots, and a bolo tie with a large tuquoise stone, enters carrying some notes.*) Señores y señoras, this is Professor Fergusson from the history department.

PROFESSOR FERGUSSON: *(Clears his throat. Stares at the audience as at a class of inattentive students.)* Los Rafas lies on a ninety-mile long depression resulting from a fault that thrust up a great block of granite whose foundation is Precambrian. It left an elongated, sediment-filled cavity. All in all, the area is relatively young geologically speaking. It was formed in the late Miocene and early Pliocene epochs, between 25 and 5 million years ago. Some unique fossils have been left behind. Trees of a kind long extinct. Giant dragonflies with a wingspread of two-and-a-half feet. Ice age animals roamed the well-watered areas . . . Just two miles north, in Pablo Griego's cornfield, we unearthed the bones of a camelops. It had a short, compact body like the South American llama, long, thin legs, and a heavy head like the modern African camel. There are several excellent specimens in the museum at the university. *(Looks toward the Stage Manager.)* How about some of Professor Krick's writings on the local weather? Rainfall. Wind velocity. Snow.

STAGE MANAGER: We're short on time, Professor. How about a few words on the history of man instead?

PROFESSOR FERGUSSON: All right . . . Paleo-Indians crossed from Siberia to Alaska and migrated south. Studies show that they were on the Río Grande about 12,000 years ago. Clovis people, early mammoth hunters, lived here between 9500 and 9000 B.C., then disappeared as did Folsom man afterwards. But people of another culture remained. Their descendants still live in pueblos only twelve miles south, with another pueblo twelve miles north. Migration of Spanish Europeans from Mexico started in the mid-sixteenth century. Some of them eventually married local Indians. The English, along with many Germans, came three hundred years later, after the Mexican War. They're still coming. These are referred to as "Anglos" by the Spanish-speaking.

STAGE MANAGER: And the population, Professor Fergusson?

PROFESSOR FERGUSSON: For Los Rafas and the farm country to the north, it's 1,007. *(Stage Manager steps forward and whispers into the professor's ear. The professor replies.)* Oh? *(He turns to the audience.)* The population of Los Rafas has just increased to 1,008 . . . For New Town, it's 11,152, of which almost 3,000 are temporary residents taking the cure for tuberculosis.

STAGE MANAGER: Muchas gracias, Professor.

PROFESSOR FERGUSSON: My pleasure, sir.

Professor Fergusson exits.

STAGE MANAGER: We've asked Señor Baca to give the political and social report. He works for the Spanish-language newspaper, *La Bandera Americana*, "The American Banner." He does just about everything there. Editor. Reporter. Typesetter. Even delivers if José Perea, Jr. gets sick. Señor Baca!

Señora Baca comes to her back door.

SEÑORA BACA: He'll be there in a minute. He got a splinter in his hand while gathering some kindling wood.

STAGE MANAGER: Thank you, Señora Baca.

SEÑORA BACA: Carlos! They're waiting.

Exit Señora Baca.

STAGE MANAGER: Señor Baca plans to buy half interest in *La Bandera* with the bonus he'll get if it ever turns a profit. But you know how small town newspapers are. Not everything that serves the public makes money.

Señor Baca enters, putting on his coat. A handkerchief is wrapped around his left hand.

SEÑOR BACA: As you all know, we're governed by a mayor and a board of aldermen representing our four wards. Los Rafas and its surrounding farms make up the Northwest Ward. All males age twenty-one and over vote. Women don't have the vote yet, although some of them influence their husbands. We're working class for the most part. Farmers with a few professional people and quite a number of illiterate laborers. Politically we're about seventy percent Republicans; almost thirty percent Democrats; maybe one percent Socialists. That's because New Mexico has been a United States territory under Republican administrations, which appoint territorial governors and hand out political spoils. We just became a state this year. As for religion, we're fifty percent Roman Catholics; forty percent Protestants; almost five percent Jewish; the rest, lost souls.

STAGE MANAGER: Anything else, Señor Baca?

SEÑOR BACA: It's a typical Western town. Not as wild and woolly as

it used to be. Gambling was outlawed five years ago. Men don't
wear guns in saloons anymore. There are no more "palaces of
forbidden pleasure" staffed by "soiled doves" who outrage
decent, church-going women. It's a lot better behaved than it
used to be. A lot duller. But our young people like it. Ninety
percent of them settle down here to live, even if they've gone
away to school someplace else.

STAGE MANAGER: (*Turns to the audience.*) Are there any questions you'd
like to ask Señor Baca?

WOMAN IN THE BALCONY: Is there still much drinking in Los Rafas?

SEÑOR BACA: There's a lot less than there used to be. There are a few
cantinas in Los Rafas, although most of the saloons are over in
New Town near the railroad tracks. By and large the farmers in
Los Rafas are a pretty sober bunch. They can't afford to get
drunk. We have a few town drunks, but they usually sober up in
time to get dragged to church on Sunday mornings. But, señora,
this is a western town. There are still cowboys and sheepmen
around. It's not exactly a dry place.

BELLIGERENT MAN IN THE FRONT: What about social—

STAGE MANAGER: Would you stand up so everyone can hear you.

BELLIGERENT MAN: What about social conditions? Poverty. Injustice.
Inequality.

SEÑOR BACA: The sheriff put down a Ku Klux Klan rally and ordered
the marchers to unmask once. And people are concerned about
who's poor. Most of the poor ones speak Spanish.

BELLIGERENT MAN: Why don't you do something about it?

He stomps out of the auditorium.

SEÑOR BACA: We try. We look for ways for the hard working and
honest to earn the necessities of life. But it isn't easy. We try to
help those who need help and mind our own business about the
others.

LADY ON THE SIDE: Señor Baca. What about culture in Los Rafas?

SEÑOR BACA: Some girls play the organ at San Felipe Church. A few
guitar players hang around the plaza picking chords instead of
doing their chores. Although there isn't much culture, we do
admire things of beauty. We marvel at the sun coming up over
the Sandía Mountains in the morning, and we're very conscious
of the weather. Farmers have a special bond with the weather.

Watching the change of seasons. Watching the rise and fall of the river. *(Affects an English accent.)* But cul—cha? You're right, señora. There isn't much. The Bible. Our waltzes and polkas. We do a lot of spirited dancing at our fandangos. And holy paintings on the walls at church. Oh, yes. There's the Passion play we put on at Easter time. It's religious, it's serious, and you could definitely call it culture.

LADY ON THE SIDE: Thank you, Señor Baca.

STAGE MANAGER: Thank you, Señor Baca. *(Señor Baca returns home.)* Now back to the plaza. Dinner is over—that's our midday meal— and the kitchens have all been cleaned. *(Señor Baca removes his coat and starts' hoeing beside his house.)* The only thing you can hear in the afternoon quiet is the sound of children from the elementary school. A few buggies on Railroad Avenue are headed toward New Town. Doc Lucero is calling on a farmer. Señor Baca is hoeing his corn patch; it rests his brain from all that work at the newspaper, besides putting food on the table. Wait. Can you hear them? The children are on their way home from school.

* * *

Antonio put aside the manuscript to rest his eyes. In his imagination he could hear the shrill girls' voices as they walked home, see the adolescent Jorge throwing his ball in the air, oblivious of his surroundings. Then Jorge and Amelia meeting and having a "real" conversation: the awkward, yearning, uncertain talk of young people still groping toward adulthood.

Like every young girl, Amelia afterwards asks her mother if she is pretty. ". . . pretty enough," she is told. Then she is ushered off to help with chores.

* * *

The Stage Manager comes to center stage. The lights dim, leaving a spotlight on him.

STAGE MANAGER: The railroad and sheep interests have just started a new bank in town. They're building it eastern style instead of southwestern adobe. They've asked Professor Fergusson what to put in the cornerstone for people to dig up in a thousand years. There's a copy of *La Bandera Americana* and a copy of the *New Town Journal*. We're including a Bible. A copy of the Constitution of the United States. A copy of William Shakespeare's plays. And, after some of us in Los Rafas raised a fuss, *Don Quixote*. Shakespeare and Miguel de Cervantes, who wrote *Don Quixote*, both died on April 23, 1661. It really makes you wonder. Here, in our own hemisphere, the great Mayan empire was once a thriving civilization. What little we know about it is mostly from three pre-Hispanic Mayan codices—painted books. In the tenth century, the civilization disappeared. Great cities were abandoned. No one knows why. As if an entire civilization had flown off to another planet. Yet before that, Mayan children sat down to supper after father came home from work. The smell of cooking blessed their homes just like here. Then empty cities. Imagine if all of our great libraries were destroyed and only three books remained of our civilization. What would historians a thousand years later know about the real lives that we lived? . . . So we're going to put a copy of this play in the cornerstone, too, so people a thousand years from now will know something real about us. More than the Treaty of Guadalupe-Hidalgo and the Spanish-American War. More than the three Mayan codices . . . So—people a thousand years from now, this is the way we lived in the great Southwest along the Río Grande at the beginning of the twentieth century. This is the way we grew up and married and lived and died.

A choir hidden from view begins singing "Holy God, We Praise Thy Name."

*   *   *

It is evening now, Antonio read. The choir at San Felipe Church is practicing. The Lucero and Baca children are doing their schoolwork. Jorge and Amelia talk quietly to each other through their open windows, as she helps him with a math problem. The bright, nearly full moon makes it almost as light as day.

The sounds of the choir grow louder. Doc Lucero calls his son,

Jorge, to talk about helping his mother chop wood. There is the sound of laughter as the ladies walk home after choir practice. They gossip about the latest scandal, the same old scandal: the choir director's drinking. The goodnights float on the moonlit air.

It is nine-thirty. Most of the lamps are out. The local deputy sheriff walks the plaza. He and Señor Baca exchange a few quiet words. The choir director walks the street, weaving slightly from his load of drink. Amelia is awake, staring out the window. She cannot sleep for the glory of the moon. Señor Baca walks in humming "Holy God, We Praise Thy Name."

In the Lucero house, María is pestering her brother.

* * *

MARIA: Did I tell you about that letter that Juana Cruz got from Sister Cecilia when Juana was sick? The address on the envelope read: Juana Cruz, Rural Delivery Box 85, San Felipe Parish, Los Rafas, Bernalillo County, Archdiocese of Santa Fe, New Mexico, United States of America—

JORGE: So? What's so great about that?

MARIA: *(Impatiently.)* Just listen. *(She continues.)* The United States of America, Continent of North America, Western Hemisphere, the Earth, the Solar System, the Universe, the Mind of God. So there!

JORGE: So?

MARIA: The postman delivered it right to her house.

JORGE: He didn't need an address. Everybody knows where Juana Cruz lives.

MARIA: Big brothers are so stupid!

STAGE MANAGER: *(Addressing the audience.)* That's the end of the first act. Go out and smoke, those who smoke. And those of you who came to please your wives and are bored, please keep your pint bottles out of sight.

Part Two

3

Morning Tribune
Monday, March 13, 1928

Descendant of Spanish Don Laid to Rest

People More Interested in New Ford Autos Than in Who Will Be Next President

"I didn't learn this all at once," Antonio began. "I probably wouldn't have believed it when I was young and innocent. Things were either good or bad, black or white then—mostly white. And as for shades of gray—well, gray isn't even a possibility when you think things are either all black or all white. But over the years I learned. About the land as well as about shades of gray.

"Of course, some of what happened I observed firsthand. Then of course, your mother, Leonor, told me more including much that she had learned from talking to, observing, and hearing about her aunt. And Leonor's father, your grandfather, filled in the gaps over the years. So it gave me a pretty good idea of what happened. What bits and pieces I didn't know I guessed from what I knew of the people and the times. So I can say that all in all it's a true story.

"But to begin with—like everything else in the state of New Mexico, the land first belonged to the Indians. When the Spanish took possession—"

"You mean stole it," Tony interrupted.

Antonio nodded.

"—our distant cousins, the rich branch of the Rafa family, received a grant that included the site for the park. After the Mexican War, the Rafas sold the ten acres to pay a lawyer to prove to the

United States government that the land on which they had lived for a hundred and fifty years was really theirs.

"The Perea family who bought it owned it until Enrique Perea died in the flu epidemic of 1918. By then the high water table caused by the Río Grande had made the land useless for farming. Dionisio Armijo bought it from Perea's widow for a price amounting to thievery.

"Armijo immediately rented it to a distant cousin, demanding payment in advance. He didn't care that the farmer couldn't make a living from it or feed his wife and six children. Then Armijo petitioned the federal government for a reclamation project to tame the river and drain the land. He could see the possibilities. The city was growing and this ten acres, halfway between Old Town Plaza and New Town, was right in the path of that growth.

"But, like in much of the West, the land found its way into a lawyer's office. It was 1928. The Roaring Twenties were just about to stop roaring and give birth to a mouse: Mickey Mouse. The United States was on the verge of the Great Depression, but nobody saw it coming. It was still country around here. Dirt roads and people trying to scratch a living from small farms. The depression wouldn't make that much difference. How much poorer could you get? How much hungrier? People just added more water to their pots of frijoles, called it bean soup, and kept on like always."

It was a very simple will, the lawyer had said. Like the late Dionisio Armijo, it was direct and plain spoken. The lawyer nodded to the two people in his plain and direct office on the second floor of the First National Bank Building.

The lawyer was dressed plainly and simply like a successful man in a conservative profession. Dark gray wool suit, the kind that itched in the desert summer. With buttoned vest and frock coat in the old style still worn by men of the old generation. His shirt collar and necktie were in the new style though. And the paunch above his belt said, "Prosperity."

The lawyer removed his steel-rimmed glasses, rubbed them on his sleeve, and looked at the man and woman on the other side of his desk. The heirs, Magdalena Armijo Sánchez Castillo Soto and her brother, Nicolás Armijo, had not exchanged so much as half a glance when they entered. They sat as if they wore blinders, stubborn mules staring straight ahead.

But they could feel each other's presence. The air vibrated with electricity ready to discharge at the slightest disagreement. With most heirs, this didn't happen until *after* the will was read. But even a will that satisfied both wouldn't have forced a pleasant word from either of them. Their hostility was of such long standing that it took the death of their father to force them into the same room.

Magdalena, tall as the average man, was not as tall as her brother, although she was huskier. She sat upright, her broad shoulders square against the back of the chair, and her long, sturdy legs firmly together. Her black mourning dress was buttoned high at the collar, setting off her dark brown hair and dark eyes flecked with gold that seemed to mirror her inner dreams.

She looked at the lawyer with intense eyes that were turned in slightly. She wasn't exactly cross-eyed. But her eyes were set in that grim face in such a way that it made you slightly dizzy when you looked her straight on. You kept shifting your gaze from one of her eyes to the other because you weren't sure which one was in focus.

"Mr. Vigil," she said in a grating voice that sent shivers down her brother's spine. Her eyes bore into the lawyer's like those of a red-neck policeman grilling a brown-faced suspect. "Get to the point. Leave out the whereases and so forths. Just tell me what it says."

She blinked with satisfaction, closing her lips firmly over her more than slightly protruding teeth. Her smile was close-lipped, and her eyes gleamed in anticipation.

"One must be professional about these things," Mr. Vigil said calmly. He placed his glasses over the bridge of his nose and carefully tucked the stems over his ears. "I, Dionisio Armijo," he began.

Nicolás, who at age forty-eight was two years older than his sister, sat rigidly still. His usually clear brown eyes were strained red and softly glistening with repressed tears. He had the slim, unworldly look of a dreamer rather than a man of practical affairs. Abruptly he reached into his hip pocket and drew out a soiled handkerchief that he quickly rubbed across the red tip of his large Roman nose. Then he tucked the handkerchief back, the move quick and sneaky like a boy in church doing something he shouldn't.

"Get on with it!" Magdalena demanded.

Vigil extended a hand for patience and continued reading, omitting not a single whereas or so forth.

"Well! What does it mean in plain English?" Magdalena asked.

"We are both his heirs equally," Nicolás said in a boyish voice somewhat subdued. He directed his comment to the lawyer as if he had not heard his sister's impatient question.

"Precisely," Mr. Vigil said. "The two of you, his surviving next of kin, are to share equally in his estate. Basically, there are ten acres of land, the savings account in Southwest Citizens Bank—a considerable sum I might add—the large house in Old—"

Magdalena shook her head vigorously. "Papá gave that to me when he got sick and asked me to take care of him." There was suspicion in her manner, and she could not decide on which of the two men to fix her stare. Was someone trying to cheat her out of what was rightfully hers? Finally, remembering, she stared at the lawyer, continuing to ignore her brother.

"I'm going by the will which is dated sixteen years ago," Vigil said.

"That's much too old. There is a newer one. Papá was always talking about changes he was going to make," Magdalena insisted. "Anyway, the house is mine. He gave it to me when he asked me to take care of him. I made him sign a paper."

Mr. Vigil shrugged. "His copy, I presume, is in the bank vault. Bring me your copy so we can submit it to the court. Mr. Armijo, do you have any knowledge of this?"

Nicolás, who had been sitting as if he were not listening, stirred and looked up from his polished but worn shoes. "Ah—I'm sorry. What was that?"

"The house in Old Town," Magdalena said in exasperation, still not looking at him.

"Yes," Nicolás said. "Father told me that he was signing it over to Maggie. She was to keep house for him and for— For—" His red eyes moistened again, and he looked away from the lawyer's stoic glance. "Leonor," Nicolás said in a tremulous whisper. Magdalena nodded with an air of superiority.

"You should go through his papers at the bank," Mr. Vigil said. "Bring any important ones to me."

"It's on file with the county recorder," Magdalena said, the matter settled.

The lawyer picked up the simple will, then another sheet which lay beside it. "To continue. The large house in Old Town which appears to have been given to his daughter, Magdalena. A 1927 Packard sedan—"

"That too," Magdalena interrupted. "That went with the house."
The lawyer turned to Nicolás who nodded.

"Various securities and notes stored in the bank vault. According
to this addendum of October 1, 1927, these consisted of one hundred
shares in Southwest Citizens Bank—"

"What?" Magdalena's voice was almost a shout. "One hundred
shares? I've been robbed!"

Mr. Vigil frowned at this latest interruption. Once again he
glanced from one to the other of the heirs, then sat thoughtfully for a
moment.

"I don't know how much you know about your father's business
affairs," Mr. Vigil finally said.

"Father never spoke to me about them," Nicolás said, "except to
say yes or no when I wanted to borrow money."

"Your father had been a client of mine for thirty years," Vigil said.
"He was one of the most astute and shrewd businessmen I have ever
met. Unfortunately, in his later years he ran into a spell of bad luck.
Ten, fifteen years ago, he was a very wealthy man. Very wealthy. But
prior to his death, he could only be described as comfortably
well-to-do.

"He made certain investments in enterprises that did not suc-
ceed." Here Nicolás turned from what he must have felt was an
accusing glance.

"The sheep business ran into difficulties and his flocks, which had
once been the largest in New Mexico, decreased. He sold his one-third
interest in Southwest Citizens Bank except for a number of shares
that he gradually disposed of over the years. He made loans that in all
honesty might never be repaid; he was a man of great loyalty to his
friends.

"The principal assets are the ten acres in Los Rafas and a substan-
tial savings account in the bank. There are other less valuable pieces
of land, plus the securities in the bank vault, but these amount to less
than ten percent of the entire estate."

"But Father was rich!" Magdalena sputtered.

"It is certainly more than I hoped for," Nicolás said.

For the first time during the meeting, Magdalena turned toward
her brother with a look of utter contempt that plainly said: It's more
than you deserve.

The look was not a surprise. Nicolás must have sensed it the way you sometimes feel a change in the atmosphere as a storm approaches across the mesa. He also turned for the first time and looked at his sister, who said, "He promised everything to me. I deserve it!"

Nicolás turned away, not in trepidation but with indifference, as if what she said was of no great importance. He had heard such declarations before. He did not believe nor disbelieve them. He never took his sister at face value. He knew her too well and whatever she said, he always asked himself: Why did she say that?

Meanwhile, the lawyer had been watching with shrewd eyes, having seen such contests unfold many times before. He interrupted at that precise moment when another word or two might have led to an angry outburst.

"We must abide by the law," he said. "The will is very explicit and, with the exception of the house and automobile, you are to share equally."

"There are two final provisions," he continued. "First, in the light of Mrs. Soto's management of the household in his later years—" Here, unspoken, or so Nicolás thought, were allusions to those several business ventures in which he had lost money borrowed from his father. "—Dionisio Armijo has asked Mrs. Soto to serve as administrator of the estate. With help as required from the officers of Southwest Citizens Bank."

"Of course," Magdalena said.

The lawyer cracked a tight-lipped smile, then droned on about other minor particulars regarding the administration of the estate.

Nicolás sat glumly, rebuked by his father in death as he had been in life. Finally, after the minor particulars droned to an end, he said, "And the other provision?"

Magdalena sat smugly indifferent as if the second provision had to be of no consequence. The lawyer cleared his throat, then continued. "In the event of either of your deaths, whatever remains of Dionisio Armijo's estate will pass on to Mr. Armijo's only grandchild, Leonor."

For the second time, brother and sister exchanged glances. "Does that mean that I don't really own my share of the estate?" Magdalena said.

'You are free to use your share with no strings attached," Mr. Vigil said. "However, if any of the estate remains at your death, it is to go to Miss Armijo. In essence, what you inherit is half share of a trust whose assets are yours to use as you see fit during your lifetime."

Nicolás smiled. There was justice after all. Magdalena stood abruptly, taller than the lawyer who had also stood. "It's mine!" she said, glowering with her slightly twisted eyes aimed somewhere between the two men so that neither of them knew whom it was that she stared at so hatefully.

She turned and rushed from the office without even a nod, slamming the door behind her so that the wall trembled.

Nicolás sat, still smiling. He looked at the lawyer who said thoughtfully, "A formidable woman that."

Nicolás nodded.

4

Evening Journal

Middle Río Grande Bill Is Signed by President

Gloria Swanson in "Sadie Thompson" at the KiMo

Knowing Magdalena, she must have seethed with anger and indignation as she rushed past the secretary and down the stairs. For a woman used to getting what she wanted, it was insufferable.

The hard click of her heels was punctuated by the angry tap of a gold-headed walking stick that had been her father's. She had only now started to carry it, convincing herself that it would be useful in protecting her from the numerous stray dogs around town. That had been her father's explanation for buying it in the first place. The 24-carat gold head was sculptured in the shape of one of the sheep that had been the source of his wealth. It was more a symbol of wealth and authority than it was a weapon against mangy curs.

She stopped outside the building and looked in both directions, temporarily confused about where the car was parked. "Here comes the señora," a voice behind her piped. "Scram!" Two small boys scurried past, casting wary glances at the walking stick that she held poised in readiness.

Juan, her Indian driver, leaned over polishing the long hood of the Packard with a rag. He was dressed in his concession to a chauffeur's uniform: faded blue jeans fastened with a leather belt whose silver buckle was studded with a large turquoise stone, a black wool shirt open at the collar, and a too-large coat from an old suit given to him by his former employer, Dionisio Armijo. This mockery of a uniform was topped by a black felt, peaked hat of the type worn by fashionable town Indians who copied the style from the latest silent movie. Or was it the other way around?

Magdalena tapped her way to the huge black sedan. "All right, Juan!" she snapped. "You'll wear it out!"

The short, stocky Indian turned his dark face in sly deference. He knew enough uppity "Spanish Americans" to hide his real feelings and play the toady. "Oh, señora. I didn't see you." Then he opened the back door and helped her in with the deference he would have shown to his feeble great-grandmother. He gave the stubborn car a more than necessary number of angry cranks, all the while cursing under his breath while smiling at the señora as if he were whispering her praises. Once behind the steering wheel, he turned nonchalantly. "Did everything go well, señora?"

"Never you mind," she said coldly. "Drive me to Golden's."

She watched nervously as Juan steered the sedan from the curb, headed east toward First Street, then north toward Golden's Market. She didn't trust him—or the car. On the less crowded street, she relaxed and sat with both hands on the head of the upright walking stick. She was lost in a vague, unfocused daydream where shadowy ghosts of thought drifted past. Suddenly she rubbed the top of the stick and jerked her head as if rudely awakened from sleep.

"He should have left it all to me," she mumbled.

"Señora?"

"Nothing. Mind your driving."

She slid her hands down the stick and stared at the burnished gold. "Oh, Papá," she sighed. "You foolish, foolish man."

Tears squeezed from the frozen eyes and dripped down the granite cheeks. She did not know if they were for her father, whom she had loved in her own way almost as much as she had feared and envied him, or for herself. Poor Magdalena, abandoned once again by the important man in her life. Left again to her own resources, while he ran off to heaven or wherever, seeking his freedom, irresponsible to the end.

Magdalena vividly remembered that morning two weeks ago. She had been brushing her hair prior to going to the kitchen for breakfast. Juan's wife, who was her housekeeper, had screamed as she ran into the house from the backyard. Her eyes had been wide with terror, and she had swallowed as if unable to breathe, pointing wordlessly out back.

What now? Magdalena had thought. A neighbor's goat trespassing again, destroying her garden? For Lupe picked the most inopportune times to go into hysterics over nothing.

"Can't you see that I'm busy?" she snapped in irritation.

But Lupe, still gasping for breath, kept jerking her arm back and forth, pointing toward the back. For the sake of a little peace, Magdalena followed her to the kitchen door.

"The ditch!" Lupe managed to gasp as they bustled along.

Lupe's annoying wheeze trailed behind Magdalena. Rays of early morning sun filtered through the trees. Just ahead, rising from the muddy brown waters, the morning star shone brightly golden, large as a hen's egg, six inches above the surface.

"There, señora. There."

Only when Magdalena had climbed the side of the ditch could she see that the morning star was the head of her father's walking stick. The other end was stuck firmly into the bottom so that the gently flowing waters did not topple it over. Puzzled, she looked down and saw the boot floating just beneath the surface. Then, extended from the boot, the pants leg of an expensive suit, no longer dry and pressed, but sagging and wavering in the quiet flow. The body was tilted at an angle, from boot downward as if the head was buried in the mud much like the lower end of the walking stick.

"Call Juan!" Magdalena croaked.

The housekeeper tottered in a circle as if uncertain in which direction to go until Magdalena pushed her roughly toward the house.

Leonor, dressed for school, came running from the kitchen. "What's the matter, Auntie?" When Magdalena did not answer, Leonor peered over the edge of the ditch, then let out a cry of, "Oh, my God!"

Magdalena stepped into the muddy water and tugged at the boot. 'Help me! We can't leave him here."

Now, looking back, Magdalena could not understand why Papá had gone out that night. He had a bottle hidden in his room, plus two cases locked in the corral. His secretiveness had been ridiculous, since she herself had bought the whiskey from the bootlegger who supplied her restaurant. But he did not want her to know that he drank as much as he did. He would even chew cloves to mask the smell of whiskey, not realizing that the aroma of cloves was a telltale sign that he had been at it heavy again.

The bottle under his bed had been two-thirds full, an excellent Canadian whiskey rather than that poisonous white lightning brewed in the mountains above the east mesa. Yet he had gone to the speakeasy behind the plaza. It would have been understandable if there had been a card game in the back room, but there had been no card game that night. Papá had not gone to lose at three-card monte as he often did.

He had wandered into the speakeasy, asking for an old political crony, then sat alone at a table like royalty on a throne, greeting old acquaintances. He hadn't stayed long enough to get drunk, really drunk, the bartender had said. Just long enough to wobble to his feet and stagger his three-legged gait out the door, leaning only a little more than usual on his gold-headed cane.

But he should have gone to the outhouse at the speakeasy, Magdalena thought. Then, when he had finally managed the half mile home, he wouldn't have needed to tightrope the planks. For he had missed the turn past the apple tree, veered left off the rude and narrow wooden bridge, apparently tried to steady himself with the walking stick, then plunged headlong into the ditch.

Even then, any fool would have simply raised himself up. To his knees even, which would have left his head and shoulders above the surface of the water. For Papá had been a tall man, and in his old age—he had been seventy-two—had shed the portly excess of prosperous middle age that would have weighed him down into the muddy bottom.

Had he been that drunk? So drunk perhaps, that even he had known it, and headed for the outhouse instead of using the chamber pot in his room? Afraid that he might be too noisy, banging the pot lid like a cymbal in a symphony orchestra? So drunk perhaps, that he had passed out, or had been barely conscious when he tumbled into the ditch?

Oh, Papá, she thought as her sorrow gave way to exasperation. It serves you right, you damned fool!

"Here we are, señora."

Magdalena looked up in surprise. It was as if she had been transported to the market by magic. She searched through her purse trying to hide her confusion.

"Here," she said, thrusting the list at Juan. "Mind that you watch the butcher when he weighs the meat."

He walked into the grocery store, thrusting his shoulders back with self-importance as if he, not his mistress, were the customer. Almost immediately Mr. Solomon Golden rushed out.

"Señora," Golden said. "I was so shocked by the news of your father. He was such a wonderful old gentleman. I want to express condolences for me and my brother, Meyer."

"Thank you."

Solomon Golden wiped his hands on his white smock, his solemn eyes watching her with concern. "If there's anything we can do. Anything. Señor Armijo was always such a friend. When you needed something done at city hall—" He spread his arms and gestured, his head thrusting forward slightly and his lips puckering in affirmation. "Let me go in and make sure they do everything up special for you. That's the least we can do." He touched her arm, then turned and hurried back into the store.

As she watched the short, stout man with the balding head disappear between the lug boxes of produce, an incident from her childhood came back to her. Old Mr. Golden had been alive then and running what had been a much smaller store. He, like his son Solomon, had been a short, stout, balding man. She and her brother Nicolás had been waiting patiently at the candy counter while old Mr. Golden waited on their mother. A new clerk, a gruff, red-faced young man, had been ignoring the children. The clerk turned and walked toward a woman who came down the aisle stopping every few feet to inspect the produce.

Nicolás had started to twist and fidget like he had to go to the bathroom, which he didn't. A timid boy, he dared not speak until the clerk had spoken to him first. As the clerk approached the woman, Nicolás began to cry. But Magdalena, incensed at being ignored, yelled out. "We were next! You're supposed to wait on us!"

The clerk looked over his shoulder with a haughty expression and continued on his way. Nicolás's tears became audible. Magdalena ran to her mother, pointing at the clerk. Mr. Golden fixed the young man with a hard stare, then waited on the children himself, refusing their money.

To Magdalena, that incident plainly showed the difference between her and Nicolás. As they had grown up, the same basic difference deepened into permanence, and her contempt for the weak-kneed Nicolás increased.

Moments later, Juan came out, arms loaded, with a young clerk following. It was much more than had been on her list, Magdalena could tell. The men stacked the bags in the front alongside the driver's seat.

"Compliments of Mr. Golden," the young man said.

Magdalena sat up even straighter, rising to a royal height, and looked down at the fair-haired young clerk as a queen to a subject. "Tell Mr. Golden thank you," she said. "I'll light a candle for him at San Felipe Church."

The clerk started to titter, covering his mouth with his fingertips. "They go to the synagogue on Seventh Street," Juan said.

"I know very well where they go. A lighted candle at San Felipe's will do them more good. Now mind your business and drive me out to Papá's land."

Juan shrugged and started the automobile, heading it west toward the newly inherited ten acres of farmland.

5

Morning Tribune

U.S. Marines Will Make War on Nicaragua

Chain Gang to Start Work at the City Parks

When Magdalena stomped from Alfonso Vigil's office, Nicolás was left with a crosscurrent of feelings. Overall, it had worked out better than he had hoped. Deep down, there had always been the fear that he would be left out of the will altogether. It would not have surprised him nor greatly upset him, since over the years his father had been more than generous in financing Nicolás's unlucky business ventures.

Mr. Vigil stood in the middle of the room until Magdalena's footsteps had faded. "Well, Nicolás," he said as he returned to his desk. "What can I do for you?" For it was obvious that Nicolás was waiting for something.

Nicolás relaxed now that only the two of them remained. He slid lower in his chair. His carefully pressed coat sleeve had started to sag, emphasizing the threadbare remains of what once had been an expensive suit. It was too bad Dionisio and he did not wear the same size. A new suit or two would have been a pleasant windfall.

"Mr. Vigil," Nicolás said, "I've signed papers in this office when father advanced me money for my enterprises. I feel that I know you and can ask a question that will not be—misunderstood."

The lawyer's face smoothed to a sleek passiveness, like a cat fully conscious that you are there but pretending you are not.

"There is this—opportunity," Nicolás continued. "You know, I work at the Wigwam Motor Court. At my age, men are used up, sucked dry. Even so, you see poor wretches at the Santa Fe shops or the lumber mill, standing in line for the menial work while strong young men get the good paying jobs. But physical work like that is out of the question for me."

Nicolás forced a shy smile. When Mr. Vigil stared impassively, Nicolás's expression turned abruptly serious. "As I said, there is this opportunity. Eddie Carr—my boss—wants to sell half interest in the Wigwam. It's on Highway 66 between here and Old Town. They say that 66 will be fully paved soon, all the way to Chicago in the east and Los Angeles in the west. And here we are, almost in the middle." His voice quickened with excitement, and his eyes shone. "It's the wave of the future. You can see what the automobile has done to this town already. Soon every family, even the poorest, will have its own Model T. And they'll all want to go motor touring."

He stopped, waiting for an enthusiastic response. Realizing after a moment that it was not to be—enthusiasm was not in the lawyer's makeup—he continued. "I'd be getting in on the ground floor of a new industry that can't go anywhere but sky high. If—I could raise the money."

"I see."

"Mr. Vigil, what are the chances—how might I go about—getting an advance from my father's estate?"

The lawyer turned and looked out the window, avoiding Nicolás's eager face. "You're asking the wrong person," he said, his words slow and ponderous. "Your sister is the executor of the estate."

"You mean I have to ask her?"

"Well, it's not that simple. By law, this has to go through the courts. Until then, the assets are frozen. There may be creditors—or debtors. There may even be other heirs, or people who think they should be heirs."

"You mean there's no way?"

"I don't mean to imply that. One might petition the court. There are times when an estate is so obviously uncomplicated that something might be done. Then again, one could use an expected inheritance for collateral for a loan. From a bank. From a private party."

"But I would have to start by talking to my sister." Mr. Vigil nodded. "You know that my sister and I do not get along."

"I would never have suspected."

"We are—how shall I put it?—cut from different cloth."

"Oh." Mr. Vigil nodded sagely.

"My sister is— No, that would be family gossip." Mr. Vigil made his first mistake and smiled. Nicolás took that as encouragement. "Let me give you an example. When we were very small, Father indulged her terribly. She was his pet. One day Father, Mother, Magdalena, and I were walking down Central Avenue shopping for a dress for Mother. I must have been six or seven years old, Magdalena two years younger.

"When we passed the display window of a clothing store, Magdalena suddenly dropped to the boardwalk. First Mother, then Father told her to get up, but she just lay there, not saying a word.

"This went on for a minute or so as people walked by and stared. Mother became angry, while Father tried to coax Magdalena into being reasonable. Finally, from where she lay on the walk, she turned and pointed silently to the display in the window: a full-length coat, muff, and tam, all of white rabbit fur, for a little girl.

" 'What is it?' Father asked. 'Do you want that little coat?'

" 'The very idea,' Mother said, trying not to look at passersby.

"When another attempt to talk Magdalena to her feet failed, Father tried to lift her, but she went so limp he was afraid she'd slither through his arms. So he walked into the store. I stood with my nose to the window, my hand shading my eyes, watching. Father and a sales clerk talked, then money changed hands, then Father was out the door with the entire outfit: coat, muff, and tam.

"Magdalena leaped to her feet with a smirk that made me want to punch her. She walked to Father, slipped her arms into the sleeves of the coat, stood still as he placed the tam on her head, then slipped her clenched fists into the muff, and looked at herself in the window. She tossed Mother and me a triumphant smile, and sashayed down the walk.

"Father laughed as if it had all been a great joke. 'That girl certainly knows what she wants,' he said, 'and knows how to get it. She's a real Armijo.'

"That," Nicolás concluded, "was and is my sister."

"Charming. Just charming," Vigil said. But his smile was mechanical and his chuckle forced. Nicolás was embarrassed, feeling foolish for revealing something that now seemed petty. He waited uncomfortably, much the way he had waited most of his life for his father to nod dismissal.

"Well," Mr. Vigil said. "I take it that's it?"

"I should speak to my sister," Nicolás said. He was disappointed and wary, not at all sure that he wanted to speak to her.

The automatic smile flashed again as Vigil stood and extended a hand. "If there's anything else I can do for you—" he said.

"Thank you. Thank you very much."

When Nicolás left, dismissed and not properly heard out, he caught the trolley and rode the short distance to the Wigwam. Eddie Carr was at the Tourists Association meeting, and Nicolás had promised to handle the desk, even though it was his day off.

It was quiet at the court. He sat by the office window, staring at the traffic moving along Highway 66 which, in the city, became Central Avenue. He was glad that Carr was away. With his boosterish energy, he would have slapped Nicolás on the back and boomed out, "Well, did you get the money?" Nicolás would have hated to answer, "Almost."

A pretty young girl walked by, reminding him of Leonor, and he felt sadder. This feeling brought him close to the depths, to the ultimate pain one suffered at family deaths. Not just for his father. Not even for his father most of all. But for the memories of those who long ago had died too soon. For his beloved wife, Mariana, and for his dear, sweet mother for whom his daughter had been named.

The telephone startled him. Reacting with nervous quickness, he almost dropped the receiver. Another traveler on the way to California. Yes, Nicolás answered. Yes. Right on the highway in the center of town. Indoor plumbing. The very latest. A café half a block away. Or, if you prefer, units with kitchenettes, especially convenient for families.

He wrote down the name, then, as he hung up, stared at the black telephone. Its insistent ring had jolted him in the same frightening way one morning two weeks ago. He could hear the insinuating voice, wary and accusing, spit out to him, "Well, he finally did it. He drank himself to death."

For the briefest moment Nicolás had not been able to identify the voice. Then, recognizing it, he still did not know who it was that finally did it. Before he could ask, the flat tin voice spat, "Papá. He's dead."

By the time he had kicked his Model T in exasperation and borrowed Eddie Carr's Chevy, the others had already arrived at the house. They hovered in a semicircle in the backyard near the ditch:

Magdalena, the weeping Leonor, the housekeeper and her husband, the doctor, a priest from nearby San Felipe Church, and a few neighbors.

Nicolás slipped to the end of the semicircle and stared at his father's body lying on the ground. Though his features had been wiped of mud, his face still resembled that of a dirty, wrinkled urchin. His new suit, which in life gave off the faint aroma of an old man who seldom changed underwear or washed, was stiffly caked with drying mud. His walking stick, wiped clean with handle polished, was in Magdalena's tight grasp, a symbol of authority. The king is dead. Long live the queen!

Nicolás was confused. Lying there, his father looked like a mischievous child who had been playing in the ditch, not like someone whose soul had flown to heaven. As for his sister's strange telephone message, what had she meant? Drank himself to death on what? Surely not ditch water.

Only later, when the doctor had signed the death certificate and the body had been moved to Ortega's Mortuary complete with change of clothes, had he pieced together what had happened. It was then, sitting in the parlor among the silent others, that a chill had come over him. For it was in that very speakeasy where Dionisio had spent his final night that Nicolás had last seen his father alive.

"Well," Dionisio had said even before Nicolás had spoken a word, "how much do you want this time?"

"Only a little, Father. Just enough to buy half interest in an exciting new business."

The old gentleman had smiled his jaundiced, wolflike grin. "You know what I like about you, Nicolás? You're such an optimist. After all the blows that life has smacked you, you still have hope."

Nicolás had flushed. Even now, remembering, he flushed. Somehow what had happened to him on his journey through life had not been personal. It had just been the way things were. Yet his father's gibe had made him feel that he was being blamed for fate's whims.

"Yes," he had answered, because he didn't know what else to say. He could not explain why he lived life hopefully. It was just the way he was.

The old man's wolflike grimace eased to one that was, for Dionisio, almost benign. "You know, Nicolás," he said in a gentle voice. "I do like you. In addition to loving you. God knows I love both my children, the others of my family, and all my friends. But you can love someone and still not like them. But I like you. Accept that as a compliment.

"Although," he said, waggling a finger, "I don't trust you with money. Not with my money. You and money repel each other. You were not meant to be a shepherd of pesos. While you are by the campfire staring at the moon or picking on your guitar, your sheep steal away. You do not even realize that they'll wind up in the wolf's belly until you are all alone by the fire and the bloodied empty sheepskins are scattered across the desert like tumbleweeds.

"Now Magdalena, I don't trust her with money either. Not that she isn't good at making it. She's almost as good as me. I don't trust her because she is a wolf, and there's no such thing as a friendly wolf. After all, they *are* my sheep.

"Then, of course, although I live with her, I do not really like her. But it is woman's work to run a household. So in my old age, it was right that my daughter should take care of me. If you had remarried, if you had a little wife of your own, well—who knows?"

Dionisio tossed down his whiskey, still smiling his benign smile, looking wistfully at his son. Nicolás, embarrassed by this rare show of warmth, turned and motioned for the bartender. He wondered if his father was secretly ill with some fatal disease and trying to close the ancient gap with affection before it was too late.

"So, what new and exciting business is it this time?" Dionisio asked. "No more schemes," he said, shaking his head in wonder and dismay, "to raise sheep on special diets?"

Nicolás frowned. He preferred not to be reminded of that one. Who would have known that his partner, a fast talking "scientist" who had furnished the ideas while Nicolás had furnished the money, would turn out to be too much of a fool to even be a fraud? Even his degree from some obscure cow college in Texas had been legitimate. He had graduated, barely, at the bottom of a class whose top scholars had proceeded headlong into bankruptcy on their family farms. The fool had actually believed that they could raise sheep with colored fleece: red, blue, green—and with varying degrees of curl. Nicolás had believed until his money ran out and the experimental herd looked just like any other herd on the mesa in spite of their more expensive, special diet.

"What is it?" Dionisio repeated. "Automobiles? The movies?" He lowered his voice to a conspiratorial whisper. "Liquor? Now there's a business for you. All the government's prohibition has done is encourage drinking. Even women. Look." He swept a palm around the speakeasy. "If they enforced the law, every man and half the women in town would be in jail."

"A motor court!" If Nicolás hadn't spoken up, the old man would have rambled on, not answering his own question and not listening to Nicolás either.

"How much?" Dionisio asked. Nicolás told him. "Let me look at the books. I can tell soon enough if it's worth it." Dionisio laid a hand on Nicolás's arm. "I'd like to see you set up before I go," he said. "I'm getting old, Nicolás. I've almost lived my four score and seven."

"Three score and ten, Father. Four score and seven is the Gettysburg Address."

"Anyway, I want to see you set up. You're a middle-aged man. Look at you. A clerk in.a tepee campsite for horseless carriages. It will never last. Get into something solid. Like ranching."

One drink later, Dionisio had agreed to advance the money from Nicolás's inheritance if the books looked good. Then Nicolás had walked the old man home through the plaza, steadying him by the arm.

"Thank you, Father," he had said when he led Dionisio to the door of the house.

The old man had shaken his head and spoken slowly, exhaling his whiskey breath. "I don't know why I like you, Nicolás. You're such a fool."

The door of the motor court office slammed. Eddie Carr's face beamed at him. "Well, did you get the money?"

"Almost," Nicolás said. "I only have to talk to my sister."

6

Evening Journal

"The modern flapper doesn't wear enough clothes to stop
an echo," Professor Paul G. Andre, chief engineer for
a Chicago loudspeaker manufacturer, complained.

Women were more virtuous then. No—no. Don't shake your
head. Not all of them maybe. But most— They knew that it was their
duty to sanctify marriage and the family and to civilize men. Although
things were changing even then. You could see a few smoking
cigarettes in public, getting drunk and loud in speakeasies, and shim-
mying like half-naked savages on dance floors.

But Leonor was a modest young lady, convent-schooled until high
school, and more modest than most. She had led a sheltered life and in
some ways was very young for her age. She was uncertain of her place
in the greater world of which she knew little. Her mother had died in
childbirth when Leonor was three years old, depriving her of parent
and sister both. The only mother she knew was her Aunt Magdalena
with whom she had lived since her real mother's death.

When she thought of her father, it was more with confusion than
with hurt or anger. He had been a traveling man since she was very
small. That's what her aunt had told her, not explaining what a
"traveling man" did besides travel. He had gone first to California,
then to Colorado, then California again, on various business "deals"
as Magdalena icily referred to them. So he wasn't able to properly raise
a daughter, although he wrote regularly, with special attention to her
birthday and certain holidays. He would appear infrequently and
without warning, then just as swiftly disappear. "Traveling" again.
Three years earlier, Nicolás had suddenly appeared again and settled
permanently in town.

One of the two constants in Leonor's life had been the lack of strong male influences. There had been rumors of at least three men in the background of the second constant in her life, Aunt Magdalena. But if they had ever existed, these "uncles" must have disappeared while Leonor was quite young, because she did not remember any of them.

Late in her young life, near the time that her father came back to stay, her grandfather, whom she had seen as rarely as her father, tired of living alone. He traded his large, comfortable house for the status of permanent resident to be cared for by Magdalena.

Grandfather Armijo now lavished attention on his only grandchild. She was suddenly the center of her father's and grandfather's concerns. Before, the only other male family members she had seen even occasionally had been her two Trujillo uncles. They were brothers of her dead mother, and Aunt Magdalena violently disapproved of them.

"Low-down Mexican trash without a pot to piss in," her aunt spat. What Leonor remembered were big, sunburnt, loud men in overalls who smelled of tobacco and sweat, argued politics, laughed at stories they whispered to each other while warily watching Magdalena, spat on the ground, and drank cheap wine.

Her most constant contact with males occurred after she left St. Vincent's Academy for girls for the public high school because Magdalena no longer wanted to pay the tuition.

There were no classes in school to explain the sudden and mysterious metamorphosis from silly schoolboy to man. It was as if a larva had magically unfolded its wings to become a full-grown insect so vastly different that one could not believe the two were different forms of the same life. She saw some similarity between her Trujillo uncles and some of the boys who teased and followed her in school. But nowhere did she see the larvae of her father and grandfather, creatures who were quite different from the coarse run-of-the-mill.

Her most persistent and strongest male influence was not from a man at all, but from the repeated warnings of her aunt. "They're all the same," Magdalena would warn. "All they want is what they can get from you."

Leonor did not know what her aunt meant. Get what? She never dared ask, and her aunt never told her.

"Liars," Magdalena would hiss. "They never tell a woman the truth. You can't believe a word they say. Remember!"

But her father and grandfather kept their promises. To Leonor's knowledge, neither of them ever told her a lie although they may have withheld the truth.

"They will cheat whenever they can," her aunt went on. "Never trust one, even when he is in your sight. He'll be plotting to take advantage of you as soon as you drop your guard."

One Sunday as Leonor sat in church, she looked up at the statues of Jesus and Saint Joseph and was struck by the realization that they were men. She was confused and torn between what her religion told her and her aunt's vague, intense, and often bitter warnings.

Her confusion reached a peak during her junior year in high school. Her own metamorphosis came unexpectedly, bringing feelings that confused and terrified her. Even if she dared, she did not know whom to ask about what she dared not admit to anyone: her vague yearnings and dreams about some young man whom she had yet to meet.

A classmate, her Trujillo cousin, was not disturbed by the dawning of romantic feelings but welcomed them. When they were little girls, Theresa María Mathilda Trujillo would hide shyly behind Leonor's older Trujillo uncle. She would look from her mended and faded gingham dress to Leonor's new starched cotton, shaking her head at her father's urgings to play with her cousin.

Now Theresa smoked cigarettes and claimed to be a flapper. She had intimate knowledge about Magdalena of which barely a whisper had ever reached Leonor. Leonor spent her afternoon trolley fare at the drugstore across from the high school while she listened to the story.

"Your aunt has been married three times," Theresa said. "Mamá told me. First, she married a Salazar, a poor relation of those rich farmers north of Old Town. She was bigger than him and used to beat him." Theresa giggled. "She nagged at him because he only worked at the sawmill and didn't make much money. Of course, he thought that she was the one with money or he would never have given her a second look."

Leonor had been shocked.

"He was introduced to her by your father," Theresa said. "They were in the war together. Not the last one but the one in Cuba."

Leonor had not even known that her father had been a soldier. He must have been wounded, she thought. That explained why he had left her with her aunt and gone off traveling. Trying to heal himself. Trying to forget.

"Everybody said your aunt married beneath her, but who else would have her? They quarreled all the time. Mostly because she never gave him any of her money. Finally it was too much. He took his army revolver and put a bullet through his head. For spite some said."

Leonor's mouth dropped open. Her spoon dripped melted ice cream onto the counter. She remembered a large, heavy black revolver that her aunt kept locked in a drawer in her room.

"Your aunt inherited a small piece of land that he owned." Theresa slurped through her straw, nodding as Leonor stared wide-eyed into the mirror, not seeing reflections of the other noisy students.

"Well," Theresa continued. "She no more got rid of one husband than she wiggled her bank book at another. My papá knew him. His name was Manuel Castillo. A sporting man. Papá used to play cards with him.

"He was a—a deceiver. Told her he had a lot of money. He used to brag about money to Papá, who knew better. But some men— The minute they got married it changed. This time he was as big as her and stronger. The first time she hit him, he hit her back. She got her gun and said that if he touched her again—" Theresa shrugged while Leonor sat stunned.

"After a year and a half trying to get money out of her, he gave up. He did manage to get her to buy that cantina, the one that's her restaurant now. That was before prohibition. Only sporting men are no good when it comes to running cantinas. They drink too much and play cards and brag off to their amigos while passing out the free drinks. Your aunt finally bribed him into an annulment and a promise to leave town. You know what an annulment is?" Leonor shook her head.

"That's when the Church says you haven't really been married. It's not like a divorce. With an annulment you can be married in the Church again."

"But—how can that be?" Leonor asked.

"If you have enough money the Church can do anything. Even make you a virgin again." Leonor was shocked. "So this guy, he left for

Arizona with a hundred dollars in cash and a check that your aunt told the bank not to pay. Can you imagine?"

"Oh, Theresa," Leonor finally said. "You're just making this up. You don't know my aunt. She's so—so cold and proper. She hates men. Absolutely hates them."

"For good reason. And you can believe me or not. But I overheard Mamá and Papá talking about it. Papá was your mamá's brother. She told him. So there."

Leonor had gone home in shock and apprehension, secretly staring at her aunt for visible signs of her history. When her father visited, she felt a terrifying and powerful constriction in her throat where questions lodged. Questions that swelled and grew and fought to break out. But she didn't dare ask her father.

She had learned about her aunt's last marriage the day they had bypassed the drug store and gone instead to Theresa's squalid little adobe house in the poor section of Barelas. Even though Theresa's parents and sisters were at work, the girls secreted themselves behind the scarred and pitted adobe walls of the corral. The goat stared at them with indifference, and the scrawny chickens cackled behind a sagging wire coop as if they expected to be fed. Theresa rolled a cigarette from a sack of store-bought tobacco, then offered it to Leonor who had determined to cross the line and smoke.

They stood beside the chicken coop, glancing nervously for signs of family or neighbors. Leonor alternately puffed and coughed as Theresa continued Magdalena's history.

"The last one," she said, "was just after you and I were born. That same year. She had this cantina that her second husband almost ruined. Luckily she hired a bartender who knew what he was doing. She became interested in him because he was a good worker, and she thought he could make money for her from the place. He liked her for the same reason the others did: she was rich.

"Well, he made a success of the cantina. But he wanted her to sign it over to him because he was doing all the work. Of course she wouldn't. Then she decided that he was cheating her. Taking from the cash box. That was when they started to have trouble. She kept trying to trap him, to find out how much he was robbing the till. But he was too shrewd, and she never caught him. Instead, they quarreled about every little thing, although money was the real reason.

"He was smart, and she couldn't control him the way she did her other dumb husbands. Finally she got desperate and filed for divorce."

Leonor exploded into a fit of coughing. She dropped the cigarette butt and ground it into the dirt. "Oh, my God," she said. "Divorce!" The most wicked of sins.

Theresa nodded. "That's not all. In order to get the divorce, she bribed him to confess to adultery."

"What's that?"

Theresa whispered in her ear while the goat watched them. "Oh, no," Leonor said.

"Yes," Theresa said. "But he held out for a price. He wanted the cantina. Your aunt was willing to suffer the shame of divorce and the anger of the priest, but she did not want to give up her business.

"Your aunt is lucky. Papá said she was meant to be rich. She finally agreed because the man had gotten nasty, and she was afraid. Then his first wife showed up. He was still married and hadn't bothered to get a divorce! He was a bigamist!"

"I think I'm going to faint," Leonor said.

"When she told him about his first wife and that she wouldn't give up the cantina, he got very angry and threatened her. That's when she went to the sheriff. Of course she made sure that one of his cronies warned him so he could get out of town.

"So you see, after three marriages she's still unmarried in the eyes of the Church. Only I think she's renounced marriage by now. She was not good with men at all."

"Oh," Leonor said, "my head is whirling. Why didn't anyone ever tell me?" Although she realized that her aunt had long been warning her about the treachery of men, and if she had had any sense, she would have known that there had to be a reason.

Theresa lifted a board from the floor of the chicken coop, brushing away the dirt, straw, and droppings, and pulled out a fruit jar. "Here," she whispered. "This is what you need." She uncapped the jar of rhubarb wine that her father made for a few special customers.

The hot liquor burned its way down, then cooled to a warm glow that made Leonor feel better. Theresa rolled another cigarette, and they stood giggling, sharing it.

"It's better for the man to be rich," Theresa whispered. "Then there isn't all that trouble. I'm going to marry a rich one."

"Tell me," Leonor said, feeling slightly silly and bold after the sips of wine. "My aunt is always saying that men are all the same. All they want is what they can get from you. What is it that they want?"

Theresa stared at her in disbelief. "Leonor, you don't know anything. Where have you been all your life?" Leonor blushed, and Theresa shook her head. "As far as your aunt is concerned, what would they want? I mean, she's old. And kind of—" Theresa puffed out her cheeks and held her arms extended in a circle that described Magdalena's size. "They want her money. After all, she's rich.

"But for someone who's young and—well, pretty—what they want is—" She wiggled coyly as if that should communicate something to her naive friend. "S . . . " she began spelling it out very slowly, "E . . . X. But then if you're married, it becomes L . . . O . . . V . . . E."

Leonor did not understand. She understood what boys wanted—within the limits of her knowledge—and had always suspected it. But the other part. That metamorphosis of S . . . E . . . X to L . . . O . . . V . . . E. That was as strange as the metamorphosis of boys to men and the awakening of her vague, delicious, guilt-provoking feelings.

Well, Leonor thought. Now I know. About Auntie. About everything! She was appalled at Theresa's knowledge of the secret, practical, unmentionable world not taught in school books. And she was dismayed by Theresa's lack of interest in things academic. Never more so than at the end of their junior year when Theresa left school to work as a domestic for an Anglo lady. Theresa had to help out at home. Work was one of the privileges of the poor.

During her senior year, having no one to share wicked and delicious times with, Leonor took the trolley straight home every afternoon. She seldom saw Theresa. When she did, her cousin, usually with a young man and smoking a cigarette, was dressed in smart clothes with one of those cute cloche hats, her stockings rolled below the knee. She was a free woman, all because she had a job and a boyfriend, and Leonor envied her.

Sometimes Peter Hubbell would follow Leonor home, begging her to stop at the drugstore with him. She wasn't interested in Peter Hubbell. His cowlick stood up like the tail feathers of a wild turkey. He punctuated every sentence with a sniff of his dripping sinuses. And when he swallowed, his Adam's apple looked like a bale of hay being hoisted to a loft.

Then one Sunday, just before Grandfather died, a chance meeting led to a change in Leonor's life.

7

Morning Tribune

Assistant D.A. Eugene Luján established a precedent for flappers and sheiks when he stated in Justice of the Peace Ritt's court that he "never put his arm around a girl in his life before he was married."

Were the times as wild then as they are now? I don't know. How do you ever know? Certainly people are more outspoken today. Whether more truthful or not, who can say? They were more private then—yes. More secretive you might say. More hypocritical? But some things should be private. What people thought about you seemed more important then—thought about your character rather than your public image, your fame—which is the word some mistakenly use when what they really mean is notoriety.

On this particular Sunday, Leonor and her aunt had just attended mass. Leonor saw her cousin Theresa across the plaza dressed in the latest style. When Theresa waved, Magdalena turned away as if she hadn't seen the girl. She took Leonor firmly by the arm and hurried her toward the car.

Magdalena had warned Leonor about her cousin. What had happened to Theresa was just what you'd expect from a girl with a coarse, ignorant father. And Magdalena berated Leonor all the way across the plaza as if it had been she who had fallen into sin.

While Magdalena did have the interests of her niece at heart, she was also worried about what people thought. In fact, that must have been on her mind most of all. She was a strange lady with strange ideas. When someone nearby smiled and cast the slightest glance toward her, she was convinced that they were laughing at her. If people nearby were whispering or talking in undertones, Magdalena knew she was the subject of their conversation. And she would react to this imaginary gossip by stiffening upright, seeming to grow even taller, trying hard to appear "proper."

She attended mass conspicuously, wanting to be seen though not to be laughed at or talked about. Going to church, she was certain, was one way to hush the rabble. Dressing elegantly was another, and she never left the house without being dressed as if going to call on the queen, even if it was only to go to the outhouse and back.

She was too self-involved to realize that people rarely talked about or laughed at her. Those few times that someone really was talking about her, it was about her ex-husbands, her money, and her too apparent hypocrisy. Spanish-speaking New Mexicans have always had a wicked sense of humor and sharp, peasant perceptions that are like needles puncturing the balloon of pomposity. Let's face it. She never fooled anyone for all her pious pretensions. But nobody cared, unless for some unfortunate reason they were subject to her power—which meant they owed her money.

And Leonor—well, she was a young girl who thought of her aunt as her mother. The two roles overlapped: aunt-mother—which somehow gave Magdalena double power over her. Leonor wanted to please her aunt. But she also wanted to see her cousin and friend, so she was torn by conflict. Like all young people, she did not know that she had the power to act on her own. Everything came from her aunt, so Auntie's word was law which she had never questioned before.

Leonor did not dare look toward Magdalena, who went on in a low, angry voice. The girl walked straight ahead, fighting hard to hold back the rebellion that was foreign to her nature. Everything her aunt said inflamed her. She knew too much about Magdalena; her aunt was no one to talk about someone else's sins.

"Do you hear me?"

"Yes, Auntie."

"That's what happens to girls who don't listen to their auntie."

"Yes, Auntie."

"I raised you to be a lady. I don't care if she is your cousin, I don't want you to see her."

Leonor did not answer. How could she? She wanted to see her cousin and friend. Theresa was fun to be with and really a nice girl. Maybe a bit imprudent. Or a bit unlucky. But, she thought, in the romantic way of young girls, wasn't that the price some paid for love?

Yet Leonor was obedient enough not to turn at Theresa's call. People still had respect for their elders then. "Do you hear me?" Magdalena repeated.

Leonor did not even nod. Her silence spoke so loudly that Magdalena stopped at the edge of the plaza and turned, blocking the girl's way. Before Magdalena spoke again, Theresa came running up, smiling shamelessly.

"I waved," Theresa said. "You didn't see me. Señora." She dropped an abrupt curtsy to Magdalena that hiked her short skirt higher above her bare knees.

Leonor did not know what to do. She turned her back to her aunt and frowned, shaking her head at Theresa. "I haven't seen you since my wedding," Theresa said. "I've been in Pecos. With my grandmother."

"We have to go," Magdalena said. "The driver is waiting." As if she ever cared a frijole whether the driver waited or not. She grasped Leonor by the arm and marched across the last stretch of plaza, but Theresa hounded after them.

"I can drive a car," Theresa said. "All by myself."

Leonor tried to twist free, but her aunt was too strong. When they reached the car, Magdalena loosened her hold to step onto the running board. Leonor turned quickly and whispered to Theresa to meet her later in the plaza. Magdalena always napped at two o'clock on Sundays, and the girls often met by the marker on the church side of the park. You know the marker, Tony—the one that makes you so mad. The memorial to a Spanish plaza, what you call a hypocritical gift to a conquered people. Given with insensitive good will by, of all people, the WASP Daughters of the American Revolution.

By now Magdalena sat on the back seat, squirming impatiently as if important things were being left undone. "Well, Juan!" she said. "What are you waiting for?"

Oh, God, Leonor thought. The queen on her throne. She barely had the strength to lift herself into the car. Only then did Leonor realize that Theresa did not know that she was being snubbed. As they drove off, she watched her cousin fade from view, all the time feeling as if she was being driven off to jail.

Leonor sat stiff and angry beside her aunt. She did not know whether or not Magdalena would continue her tirade. That was not always her way once she got what she wanted. Sometimes there would be cold silence that drove the girl's thoughts back onto themselves, back onto all that her aunt had done for her. All the sacrifices that Magdalena endlessly reminded her of as signs of her—not love, Magdalena could not bear to speak the word—but of her duty, her responsibility, her generosity. It was charity above and beyond what was necessary. That's what her aunt implied. But to Leonor it was a giant hand that stilled what independence and willfulness she occasionally felt, not with a loving touch, not even with a blow, but with a firm heavy restraint that was punishing to the extent that she fought against it.

As the car cruised from the plaza, spinning up dust as it drove past adobe houses, Leonor glanced wistfully at the square little house that she still thought of as home. It was where she had been taken when her mother died, where she had lived until three years ago when Magdalena had triumphantly taken possession of Grandfather's large house that was closer to New Town.

Today, driving past that house was like saying goodbye to her girlhood, to her innocence. The seed of rebellion that had always lain dormant deep inside had been watered and fertilized by what she had learned about her aunt. She not only questioned Magdalena's pronouncements and warnings for the first time—though silently—but also saw with open eyes her aunt's hypocrisy. Magdalena had never once mentioned or even hinted at three ex-husbands.

At first Leonor did not hear the deep, cold voice, its loud whisper restrained so that Juan would not hear, although he heard everything, even the silences. The girl turned, seeing the granite face staring straight ahead, the statue's lips moving in a warning to her though aimed toward the front of the car.

"That girl *had* to get married. Do you know that? It was a scandal all over town."

Leonor turned away. She did not want to hear. She had been at Theresa's small, private, and quickly arranged wedding. Had been one of the bridesmaids, while Theresa's sisters had served as the other bridesmaids, and her madrina, her godmother, had been matron of honor.

Though Theresa had said nothing, Leonor had known that the wedding was not the joyous occasion it should have been. It was treated as an anxiously hushed secret, hurriedly whispered in order for it to fade all the more quickly. Then she had heard that her cousin had been in the hospital. Shortly after, the gossip went, Theresa had been sent north to her grandmother's.

"I don't want you to see her," came the insistent whisper. "What will people think?"

"She's my cousin. My mother and her father were sister and brother."

"All the more reason. People will say it runs in the family."

What runs in the family? Leonor wanted to shout. But she dared not. She knew her aunt's tone of voice. The matter was settled.

Grandfather, dressed in suit and tie, was sitting in the sunshine on the screened front porch when they arrived. He nodded and smiled at Leonor, who kissed him on the cheek, hardly noticing the faint aroma of urine and stale sweat that was, she thought, the usual fragrance of old people; the way mothers smelled faintly of white flour and green chili, and babies smelled of sour milk and dirty diapers.

"Have Juan drive you to church!" Magdalena snapped at her father.

"¡A la chingada!" the old man answered.

Leonor left the porch quickly, her heart starting to race, for she knew what was coming: another of their quarrels. She closed the door to her room, still hearing the angry voices from the porch. Then rapid footsteps passed through the sala to the kitchen. Once again quarrelsome voices. This time Magdalena carped at Lupe about dinner.

Leonor would not leave her room while her aunt marched through the house setting everybody and everything straight. She opened a schoolbook, such was the depth of her boredom. But even Spanish, her favorite subject, held no appeal. She stretched out on her bed, the book open but unread, and wondered about her cousin Theresa and about her dead mother who had been Theresa's aunt.

It runs in the family, she said to herself, puzzled. She stretched over to the bureau that stood crowded next to the bed. She reached on top without looking, fumbled about, then lifted a small, gilt-framed photograph: her mother. She turned it over and read the inked inscription: Mariana Trujillo Armijo, 1914. The year Mother had died.

Leonor stared at the youthful face smiling from the brown tinted photograph. What was it that ran in the family? She saw the pretty face of a young woman only a few years older than herself. The hair was dark and shiny like her own. The eyes—it was hard to tell about the eyes in a sepia photograph—except that they must have been brown. But the mouth and smile were so astonishingly like looking at herself or even at her cousin Theresa, that Leonor sat up and stretched toward the mirror above the bureau. She pursed her lips, full and faintly blushed—her aunt would not let her use much lipstick. Then she stared back at the photograph. They were perfect cupid's bow lips, just like her own. She smiled. Wasn't that what movie stars had? Wasn't that what ladies' magazines insisted was the ideal? Nice full lips, naturally pursed, on the verge of a kiss. That's what men admired.

She thought of her cousin Theresa who *had* to marry José Rafa. Theresa had said that she planned to marry a rich man. She had—sort of. At least José's family still owned land in the area where they had once owned so much. But then the shame of having to get married and everybody knowing about it. Theresa had never spoken to her about that.

What runs in the family? She looked suspiciously at her mother's photograph. Had she, Leonor, been a love child? Was that why her father had left her with her aunt and gone traveling? Was she somehow to blame for her mother's death? Had Mother died of shame and remorse for this dishonor?

Leonor closed her eyes and shook her head violently. "No," she whispered, on the verge of tears. "Not *my* mother. *Not me!*"

There was a rap on the door, and Lupe announced dinner. Leonor sighed and put the photograph back on the bureau. If only there were someone to talk to, she thought. But there wasn't. Certainly not her aunt. And not her father or her grandfather—they were men. Perhaps Theresa, she thought. Only what would she know? She had already ruined her own life.

The midday meal was quiet, as if the quarrel had exhausted Magdalena and her grandfather. Magdalena carved the roast chicken and served. Grandfather sat with watery eyes gleaming as Auntie passed the plates. Lupe walked back and forth from the kitchen, carrying away empty dishes, bringing in hot tortillas, refilling the water pitcher, doing the quiet biddings of her mistress. It was as if all of them were trying to make up for their previous quarreling.

After dinner, Grandfather fell asleep on the porch, snoring. Magdalena went to her room. Leonor told Lupe that she was going for a walk, then hurried the half mile to Old Town plaza.

There was no one in the square when she arrived. She waited on the grass near the market, looking around anxiously. Then she heard a call and turned to see Theresa leaving church.

"Oh," Theresa said. "I have so much to tell you. You know," and she was solemn and serious, a Theresa that Leonor seldom saw. "I lost my baby." Then her pretty face puckered and shriveled and tears streamed down her cheeks. "Oh, Leonor. It's so sad."

Leonor embraced her. She listened, forgetting her own problems, her own questions, until a shiny little Chevrolet chugged into the plaza, tooting its horn.

"There's José," Theresa said, wiping her eyes. "You'll have to go out with us some time. Do you have a boyfriend?"

Leonor shook her head, flushing in embarrassment. José, dressed in his dark Sunday suit with a cap on his head, stepped from the parked car and waved. A smiling young man dismounted from the other side of the car and walked toward the girls. Oh, how very collegiate he looked, with his flannel trousers and a white sweater that only swells wore. His hair was parted in the middle and slicked straight back just like a sheik's. Oh, my, Leonor thought. He's the cat's pajamas. She could barely speak when they came up, beaming, and José said, "Leonor. This is my cousin, Tony."

8

Evening Journal

Fall Agrees to Tell Teapot Dome Story

Tom Mix in City En Route Via Gas Bus

When Father died, Nicolás considered, he left the big house near Old Town completely furnished and paid for; the year-old Packard sedan, one of the finest cars in the state of New Mexico; ten acres of choice land between Old Town and New Town; several tens of thousands of dollars in Southwest Citizens Bank; a few pieces of high desert property; miscellaneous securities—and my sister, Magdalena. Which was why he felt uneasy as he stood inside the screened porch of the house.

He also had an uncanny feeling that his father was still there, sitting on the wooden rocking chair, staring at the road. He thought he heard the rocker squeak and quickly turned, half expecting to see Dionisio's ghost watching him doubtfully as if asking, Do you really think you can handle her now?

But the rocker was still, as still as the silent morning that was finally stirred to life by footsteps approaching the door. Other brothers might burst into their sisters' houses without knocking—few locked their doors since visitors were usually relatives or neighbors—but not Nicolás.

"Is she in?" he asked Lupe.

But Magdalena was at the café, so he left, waving at Juan who was in back polishing the car. "Well, patrón," Juan said. "Do you think she'll finally get indoor plumbing after . . . this?" He meant the old man's death. If the house had had indoor plumbing, old Dionisio might still be alive.

"Sometimes people resist progress," Nicolás shrugged. "If I bring my car over Sunday, will you polish it?"

"Pues sí, señor."

The café was in an adobe building a short distance from Old Town plaza. He parked on the square and made his way down a narrow alley. The door was locked—it did not open for business until eleven o'clock—so he knocked until the cook let him in. Magdalena was seated at a table near the cash register.

He pulled out a chair and sat across from her, looking around and sniffing the air that smelled suspiciously like liquor. She continued studying a list without giving him a glance, then finally looked up with suspicion. "Well, what do you want? Can't you see that I'm busy?"

"Are you doing business after hours?" He sniffed the air again. "Good stuff, too." When she glowered at him, he asked, "Where's Leonor?"

"She'd better be in school."

Nicolás's body tightened involuntarily. A pain stabbed him between the shoulders, and his breathing quickened. The lump in his chest weighed him down, and it was all he could do not to shout curses at her because of her overbearing manner.

"Well," she finally said, as if swatting at a fly that was annoying her. "How much do you want now? Whatever it is, you won't get it."

"I want to talk about the will."

"I can't. I'm busy."

The hostility flowed from her in waves, and his silent anger rose to meet it. "I have a chance to buy half interest in the Wigwam. I spoke to Dionisio the week before he died. He was going to arrange a loan through his lawyer, but he never got around to it."

"How do I know you're telling the truth?"

The question didn't deserve an answer. "Vigil says that an advance could be made from the estate. From the cash in the bank. Only you're the executor so it would need your approval."

A cruel smile crossed her lips, and her eyes gleamed with a sense of pleasure, a sense of power. He knew that look. She was going to get him. Get him good.

"Well," she said sweetly in a sudden flip-flop of attitude, "until the estate goes through the courts, we really can't touch it, can we? There may be claims or—who knows? I'm sorry. We should really go by the rules."

He did not know why he continued talking, continued trying to persuade her. It was futile. He knew it even before he had asked the question. But he raced on anxiously, talking faster and faster, about how all it required was a petition and her approval. That the loan was less than one-quarter of his share of the cash. That it was an opportunity *now*, and might never come up again. But the more he talked, the more pleased the expression on her face and the more gentle her refusal. She knew she had him, and she was enjoying it.

"We'll just have to wait," she said. "The estate isn't settled. Who knows what will happen?"

The pain between his shoulders collapsed into a vicious knot. The lump in his chest opened like a knife wound, hot and deep. He sensed the warning in her words. "What do you mean who knows what will happen?"

She looked at him in surprise and innocence. "Why—who knows?"

But he knew that look too. How often in their childhood had she assumed that look after provoking him to anger, after she had struck the first blow and he stood with his fist raised while his father entered the room to catch him picking on his poor little sister? It had been a way of life, the surprise and innocence that exacted double from him: first her blow that caused him more anger than pain, then his father's punishment, a whipping for hitting his innocent little sister.

Until that time when they were older, when for once Father had been out of her view when she started her provocation that had ended with a vicious kick to his groin. He had doubled over, screaming, while her triumphant look turned to one of fear because he had never screamed like that before. Even then Father had waited to see Nicolás finally straighten up and rush at Magdalena with an urge to kill.

"Papá!" she screamed. "Nicolás is going to hit me!"

Father had stepped out from behind the door where it was obvious he had been watching. Magdalena had looked up in shock, while Nicolás had come to a halt and lowered his fist, waiting for the blow from his father.

But the blow never came. Instead, Father towered over them and said sternly, with suppressed anger to Magdalena, "Never kick a man there!" Then to both of them, "I'm tired of your fighting. I want this settled once and for all." Then to Nicolás. "All right. Go ahead." And

Father had drawn back while Nicolás, surprised, had thrown a feeble fist at his sister. When she retaliated with a kick to the shins, he had pummeled her, all his resentment and anger at last receiving satisfaction. That had been the last time they had ever come to blows.

Magdalena shuffled the papers on the dining table, in no hurry to return to her work. "You know what dear Papá would say," she continued. "He worked so hard and sacrificed so much for us. It would be an abuse to his memory not to go by the rules, by the law."

But Nicolás remembered too well what Father had thought of the law. He had owed much of his success in territorial politics to "voting the sheep." For years he had controlled the rural district south of here where he pastured most of his flocks. Every sheep had been given a name that was entered into the voting rolls before each election. Victory was always assured. Until that final election when there had been more votes than people in the district and Dionisio had been driven out of politics in a scandal. He had been forced to resign from his party's national committee and had been replaced by someone else who could deliver the Hispanic vote.

"I dreamed about Papá last night," Magdalena said. "He told me that he was happy and that I should look after his interests."

"What interests would a dead man have?" Nicolás crossed himself, not so much from superstition as from caution.

"His will."

Nicolás was incredulous. "He came to you in a dream and told you to look after his will? You mean like the time after Mother died when she appeared to you in a cornfield in her First Communion dress and told you that the only thing she missed in heaven was being near you?"

"I was Papá's favorite," she retorted. "And Mother's too. There is something between mother and daughter, between women that—"

Yes, he remembered: something that men will never understand. But he remembered their mother, Leonor, too well. She had been an old-fashioned, silent woman, who cooked and kept house while her husband was out conquering the world. Magdalena had ridiculed her dutiful mother, who had been neglected and occasionally mistreated by her husband. Yet Mother had borne it without resentment or complaint, had gone to church every day and seemed to forgive whatever trespasses came her way. "Gutless," Magdalena had called her. Yet Mother had been fair to her daughter, even though, Nicolás suspected, she had never really liked her. Or perhaps Mother had been too involved in her own small world of duty and church to do other than tolerate her father-spoiled daughter. As for Nicolás, Mother had always tried to protect him from his father's anger, showing to her son what little affection escaped the bounds of her stoic exterior.

"This dream of yours," he said, "it wasn't like the time that Father came back to you as a cockroach?"

"I'm busy," she answered coldly. "This café does not run itself. You've heard my answer. No. The estate has to go through the courts."

Magdalena turned to her papers. Nicolás saw the cook and waitress huddled together in a corner watching her apprehensively. Then the waitress rolled her eyes toward the ceiling and shook her head.

Nicolás left with the uncomfortable feeling that he was in her power. Exactly where she liked people to be, and exactly where he had vowed he would never be again.

9

Morning Tribune

"Women Must Keep Illusions about Men and Acquire Them for Each Other," Says Dr. Florence Mae Morse

Chaves County Woman Wins State Senate Berth

Magdalena did not acknowledge the word "love." It was not in her vocabulary. She knew honor, and she knew obey—oh, how she knew obey. She had learned that from the very first, from her father, who had ruled her childhood home like a despot, whose moods flashed from one extreme to the other with dizzying rapidity and little provocation. It had confused and terrified her stoic and dutiful mother, why shouldn't it have confused the little girl?

The way to survive, Magdalena had learned, was to smile and to please. To cater, hiding what she truly felt and repressing her true and aggressive nature. If Father was pleased, he would in turn please her, that is give her what she wanted. Even an occasional spark of assertiveness could please Father. As long as it was not too frequent and was not directed at him. He would laugh and slap his thigh, turning to her mother in admiration of this daughter of his. Wasn't she something?

But Magdalena paid a heavy price. She had grown up in a time when women knew their place, and that was as helpmates to men. The gap between what she felt and how she acted was charged with tension. It was as if, in not being true to her own nature, she had comdemned herself. It was a common enough dilemma, deciding which way to lose in the age-old battle of the sexes. It left her with constant and gnawing anxiety, with an overwhelming insecurity that she could only equate with living in hell. For her, hell was waiting for you-know-not-what to happen you-know-not-when.

She had decided early, slyly watching the daily interplay of her parents' so-called typical marriage, that to be like her mother was to commit herself to a form of slavery. To be the master she had to be like her father, like all men—almost all men, she reconsidered, thinking of her brother. And if one had not been born a man, one must all the more learn men's tricks to persevere and make one's way.

Her childhood school for war had been daily life. The enemy had been her brother. She thought it would be enough to learn to deal with men by learning how to defeat this one standard bearer who did not even know he was in a war. But the stakes were raised when she saw that she who should have been her staunchest ally, her mother, instead favored Nicolás, who spent his boyhood sniffling at the martinet voice and militant hand of their father. The sympathy, the embraces, the rare kisses, flowed out to him, while she, the dutiful daughter, existed at arm's length from this traitorous member of her own sex. It spurred Magdalena to engage in battle with added determination, with constant and intense vigor, because by winning, she hoped to bring her traitorous mother back to the fold where she belonged.

When finally, at school age, Magdalena had been thrust into the world outside, she found herself at a loss. It did not conform to the sheltered castle at home where she was the king's favorite. Someone had changed the rules. Willfulness, of course, was not tolerated. And the game was no longer to make someone else look bad. The game was to look good as the result of your own efforts. That was difficult for her. Being lovable, trying to please were difficult enough. But in schoolwork, one had to *know* what one was doing. Here her obedient, soul-eyed brother did well, while the alphabet, numbers, and facts did not surrender to her petulance and suppressed willfulness. One had to surrender to them to master them, and she would surrender to nothing or to no one.

Magdalena was not particularly well liked by her classmates. Her high-handed ways, repressed among adults, were unleashed when among peers. The other girls did not care for her. She was selfish. She was stuck-up. She wasn't very pretty. And they didn't care if her father was rich and a political boss.

Later, when there were important social events at school, boys did not ask her out. Rejected, she rationalized that she was too good for them. They were just a bunch of dumb farmers. Stupid shit kickers. But that did not salve the pain of being left out, of not taking part in the good times. She went alone to one school dance, but it was too humiliating. She felt an overwhelming revulsion for the few clods who mumbled at her and whom she refused to join on the dance floor. Why didn't one of the handsome, popular boys ask her? But they didn't. And after a night that lasted a thousand years, she renounced dances for ever.

Nevertheless, there was still the senior dance the last year of school. Nicolás, home on leave from the army, was bullied into taking her and her girlfriend. He bribed one of his army cronies to squire his sister while he escorted his sister's friend. And it was Nicolás, having served out his enlistment which included a brief foray into Cuba with the Rough Riders, who introduced her to another drifting army veteran, Alonso Salazar, the year after her graduation.

Magdalena was already referred to in whispers as an old maid. In the old days Hispanic girls often married when they were fourteen or fifteen years old. She was working in the bank of which her father was cofounder and was also helping Dionisio with other business when Alonso appeared in her life.

One morning Nicolás walked in, dirty and smelling of the sheep camp from which he had ridden that day, to change a twenty-dollar bill. The short slender young man with him had stood with a silly smile on his face, waiting to get his own change. His lecherous eyes massaged her tall and stately body, and she felt anger and confusion.

"You remember Alonso," Nicolás said. "We were in the army together."

She didn't remember Alonso. She had never met him before. But she nodded stiffly, trying to ignore the look whose meaning she understood only too well. He was a cute little thing, but he still made her very uncomfortable.

"A lady banker," Alonso had said. "How nice."

That was how it had started. With visits to the bank, first the two of them together, then Alonso alone. Until the two men had quit the sheep camp because it interfered with their carousing in town, and Alonso had taken a job at the local lumber mill.

Alonso Salazar was one of the distant, poor relations of the Salazars who owned property north of Old Town and were political allies of her father. The name was right. It was the bank account that was wrong. But there was a simple playfulness about Alonso that pleased her. Like having a puppy follow her around. And she felt that he was no threat. He bowed to her superior intelligence and assertiveness, letting her have her own way.

She wasn't really marrying beneath her, Magdalena rationalized when he finally proposed. Salazar was a good New Mexican name. He had inherited a small plot from his father, enough for corn, tomatoes, chili, and the little adobe house that they would call home. Her dowry was a generous cash gift from Dionisio that immediately went into the bank.

The true nature of their marriage revealed itself the first time Alonso asked for money. The taxes were due on the property. They quarreled not just because of that, but because taxes were still due from the previous two years. The tax collector threatened to confiscate the land if they did not pay. Then other overdue bills found their way to her, and they quarreled over these. About his gambling debts, his drinking. She did not pay the debts, holding tightly onto her dowry and doling out what she earned at the bank begrudgingly. He was the man. He was supposed to support his wife. What the hell did he do with what he earned at the sawmill?

Alonso could not understand why she didn't use some of her own money so they could live better. What was she saving it for? Finally, after endless quarrels during the year and a half of their marriage, he got even with her. Displaying the latent instability that occasionally showed itself in the headstrong Salazars, he went out early one morning. He fed the chickens, chopped some wood and stacked it neatly by the back door, then took his army revolver from his waistband and put a bullet through his head, ending the marriage. So there!

After the initial shock, the horror of blood and flesh splattered on the wall of the corral, the agony of explaining to family and neighbors, she said to herself: "Good riddance!" It was more a blow to her ego than a personal loss. A rejection, as if her marriage had been a high school social where no one asked her to dance. But this rejection had its rewards: the small piece of property that had belonged to her husband was now hers.

Her one regret did not surface until much later, growing from an uncomfortable and undefined sense of lack. Only after her second marriage had failed did she realize what this feeling was: she did not have a child of her own. That was all that any husband, any man, could give her, and one of the reasons, after two failed marriages, that she dared try again.

But third times are not always charms, so after the third failure, she renounced men and marriage forever, though still obsessed with the great lack in her life: a child.

She watched with jealousy as her ineffectual brother sired a daughter within a year of his marriage. Watched with not a little pleasure as his wife lost another child a year and a half later. Then somehow sensed with the primitive instincts of a predator when her sister-in-law died in childbirth two years after that, that an opportunity was beckoning. It was not unlike the realization after her first husband had put a bullet through his head: someone else's misfortune would be her own good luck.

Magdalena moved in quietly, under the guise of helping Nicolás, whose work at the bank suffered from the unbearable shock of his wife's death. "Let me take care of Leonor for you," she cooed. "A baby needs a woman's touch."

She gradually took over Leonor's upbringing, finally moving the baby to her own house "for her own good." She had long since lost her job at the bank when her father sold much of his share to prop his faltering sheep business. She had not gotten along with the new owners. Now, with a baby to raise, she had something to do with the unoccupied time and abundant energy that would otherwise have driven her mad. By relieving Nicolás of the responsibilities of parenthood, she left him free to drown his sorrows in drink or pursue some crackpot business if he could talk Dionisio into another loan.

Before long, Nicolás went to California to start a new life and "seek his fortune," promising to send for Leonor. He at least found employment. He worked as an extra in the new and exciting field of motion pictures, turning his agility on horseback and his dark looks into a myriad of brief, flashing appearances on the screen among a horde of other similar young men chasing the settlers or raiding the wagon train. In between parts, he worked as a waiter in a Hollywood restaurant.

In a year, Nicolás had, as he wrote in one of his weekly letters: "gotten the bad luck out of my system." He was ready to take Leonor, not, as Magdalena supposed, because he had found another wife. He could not imagine making that sacred commitment to anyone else. As far as he was concerned, he was married for eternity to his dear, dead Mariana. It was, in fact, those very feelings about Mariana and the tender memory of his dead mother for whom their daughter had been named, that drove him to vow to care for her himself. He owed that to the blessed women in his life.

Magdalena ignored his letters. If she did not answer, she thought, he would stop writing. He would forget this crazy idea of taking back Leonor. The baby was Magdalena's now! More her daughter than his.

Nicolás did stop writing. One week, instead of a letter, an angry Nicolás appeared. He had given up a supporting role as a bandito in a forthcoming western, his first big chance. Even turned down a screen test for a major role. Latin lovers were in vogue. The studio wanted to groom someone to compete with that Italian in the burnoose, and it was a great opportunity. But his daughter was more important. He wanted his daughter!

Magdalena tried to resolve the dilemma the only way she knew. Using the same bargaining power with which she had enticed and won three husbands. By offering to buy the girl. Nicolás was outraged. "Do you think a baby is a hen in a cage at the butcher shop? If you want to buy a human being," he shouted, "there are plenty of unwed mothers who would be glad to sell you one. But not me!"

His outburst terrified her. She retreated, seeking another way. Without telling Nicolás, she saw a lawyer and started proceedings against him for abandoning his daughter, insisting that she should have legal custody. The judge who was to hear the case owed his position to Dionisio Armijo, and he told his patron. The suit was quietly killed. Dionisio warned Magdalena in no uncertain terms that if she ever tried such a thing again, he would cut her completely and irrevocably out of his will. She gave in because he had spoken her language.

Her attempt had alerted their father. For the first time, Dionisio considered the question of his granddaughter. An unmarried Nicolás who had difficulty caring for himself was hardly the person to raise his granddaughter. There were many advantages to Magdalena raising Leonor. Perhaps Nicolás could move in with her or, barring that, move in with Dionisio in the large house that had been empty since Nicolás's mother's death. But Nicolás would have none of it.

Only after Magdalena had skillfully encouraged Dionisio to

finance one of Nicolás's business schemes did Nicolás compromise. Instead of taking Leonor, he rented a small house close by so he could see his daughter every day.

Knowing his changeability, Magdalena was content to wait. If her brother was busy trying to raise sheep with colored wool, she reasoned, he would not have time to raise a daughter, nor lurk about waiting to kidnap her and take her to California.

Magdalena continued to raise Leonor. Nicolás pursued his venture, living in his own little house. As time passed, Magdalena was for all practical purposes her niece's guardian. It was not long before Nicolás's business took him to Colorado. Then, when the venture failed, he returned to California, no longer driven by the urgency to have his daughter, since she was well taken care of and he was free to see her whenever he wanted.

As for Magdalena, she accepted what existed in fact—that Leonor was hers—without having to certify it in law. Time and Nicolás's changeability had resolved the situation. It worked more comfortably that way. If she did not confront him about legal possession of the girl, he did not feel threatened and, in turn, threaten to take Leonor from her.

Thus, when Nicolás made the last of his many moves back to Albuquerque, there was no conflict about the girl who by this time was in high school. She was her own person now—almost. Something that Nicolás accepted with good grace and that Magdalena resisted, turning from the tug-of-war in which she had contested her brother to this new tug-of-war with her niece.

10

Popular song

**"I'm blue ev'ry Monday,
Thinking over Sunday,
That one day when I'm with you."**

Antonio had waited near the bandstand in Old Town plaza.
Theresa had told him that Leonor and her aunt attended the eight
o'clock mass. He could still remember it—the cold April morning,
services already begun, and she hadn't appeared. His hands were
thrust deep in his pockets, his coat collar turned up. He waited
through mass until the church emptied, seeing only José and Theresa.

"Your nose is red," Theresa said. "Have you been waiting in the
cold?" She smiled her sly smile. "Or did you take the hair of the dog
this morning?"

Antonio muttered some kind of silly denial. He looked to José for
help, not daring to say a word because Theresa would tease him. Then
the deep throb of an automobile shook the earth. Ten thousand
needles jabbed his skin, and his hair tried to stand on end. Before he
could catch himself, he turned and stared at the black Packard sedan
coasting solemnly to a halt as if it were leading the procession to the
communion rail.

"I see," José said.

Antonio watched silently and intensely as the Indian driver
opened the rear door and the two black-garbed women dismounted.
Leonor glanced cautiously as she walked past the bandstand, lifting a
hand at Theresa.

Antonio could barely catch his breath. Even in mourning clothes,
black from hat to gloves to shoes, her appearance unsettled him. He

watched with a mixture of guilt and reverence as the folds of her coat pressed against her body. She was small and modest in manner, seemingly unaware of her beauty. He felt like a voyeur, almost obscene, confused by the odd mix of worship and attraction that overpowered him.

"I think," José said to Theresa, "that a tribe of cherubs with bows and arrows have shot Tony right where it hurts."

Antonio turned abruptly after Leonor entered the church. His friends' knowing smiles embarrassed him.

"I already introduced you," Theresa said. "Did you get her telephone number?" Antonio shook his head. "You want me to fix you up? We could all go to the dance at the social hall next Saturday." When he didn't answer, too confused and embarrassed, Theresa tried again. "Or the party next week. Whose party, José?"

"Billy Hammock's."

"Yes. It's his twenty-first birthday. I could fix it up."

Antonio remained speechless, thunderstruck. José shook his head in mock disgust. "Give him her telephone number. My God, Tony. You'd think you'd never seen a pretty girl before."

"Pretty? She's—she's—"

Theresa took out her lipstick and scribbled on a scrap of paper. "There. Don't fold it or it will smear. Her aunt takes a nap Sunday afternoons. You should take her for a drive."

She and José exchanged smiles. Antonio grabbed the scrap of paper as if it would fly away. "I have to go to mass," he said abruptly.

He could feel their eyes boring between his shoulder blades, see their lips twisted in knowing smiles. He hurried across the square and into the church, standing behind the last pew searching until he saw her. Then he moved to the pew directly behind her. He was so close he was enveloped by her scent. What was it? Lilac? Yes, he thought with delight. She exhales lilac and the pores of her smooth, soft skin exude a film of rose water.

During mass he knelt when he should have been sitting, sat when he should have been on his feet. He started to sing the wrong hymn in a loud, brash voice until a little boy in the pew in front turned and a woman beside him put a hand to her mouth to cut off a snicker. Once, when he should have been sitting but was kneeling, he could barely keep from burying his face in Leonor's soft, dark hair. The sound of worshipers rising startled him, and he stood, joining the others.

When mass was over and the congregation filed from the pews, she turned. Her eyes brightened in surprise, and she smiled. Antonio's day was already a success.

He waited, resisting the rude nudge of the woman behind him, so he could follow Leonor and speak to her. He burst from the crowded church as if from a prison, his heart pounding. He rushed toward Leonor, ignoring her aunt who turned a disapproving face without breaking stride.

"What a surprise to see you!" he said.

She smiled. He knew that she was not deceived. "Auntie," she said. "This is Mr. Rafa."

Magdalena looked him up and down, her expression frozen, as she increased her speed. Antonio smiled gallantly at her wordless grunt as if it were a pleasantry or an invitation.

"Will you be at home this afternoon?" he asked Leonor. "I'd like to come by and pay my respects."

He felt foolish at his stilted words, while Leonor turned a frightened and troubled face toward her aunt who uttered another more forceful grunt. Leonor quickly turned back and nodded at him.

"Two o'clock?" he asked in a low voice, hoping that Magdalena would not hear. Again Leonor nodded, flickering a timid smile. He stopped at the edge of the square and watched them cross the dirt road.

The driver held the rear door open as they boarded, glancing at Antonio with an expressionless face. As Antonio stared, Leonor turned, more composed now, and rewarded him with a smile. He could not restrain himself. He leaped in the air and clicked his heels together, unaware of the parishioners passing by.

*   *   *

"Just exactly what is it that you do, young man?"

Magdalena's suspicious eyes bored into him. Her voice and the set of her mouth put him off. There was a twist, a haughty quality of disbelief in the way she said the most commonplace words. It kept repeating its silent message: I don't believe you. What are you up to? Don't think you can fool me.

"Why—I want to get on in the modern world. To take part in progress. To—to get off the farm on the road to the future."

Magdalena all but rolled her eyes at this pomposity. Antonio was suddenly aware of how it must have sounded, and his face turned bright red.

"Yes," Magdalena said smugly, "but what are you? A farmer? A teacher? Anything at all?"

Leonor sat uncomfortably on the other side of her aunt who had placed herself between the young people as if without her presence they would immediately rush into the most shameful and lascivious behavior on the horsehair sofa or—God forbid—on the floor. Leonor sighed and smiled timidly at Antonio. It reassured him.

"Have you heard of the Sandía Creamery in the south valley? My father is foreman. But I don't want to be a dairy farmer. I want to move up in the modern world.

"I went to Vegas Normal School for two years, but after teaching part-time in Tijeras Canyon, I decided that it wasn't for me.

"There were twenty students," he said. He was talking to Leonor now, aiming past her aunt to the young woman who watched him with interest. "All in one room. Some of them were as old as me—and bigger. Others were barely out of diapers, if they could afford diapers.

"Some of them barely knew English, so I had to teach part of the time in Spanish and part of the time in inglés. To keep order I got in good with their leader, the biggest young man in the class. One day I got angry and invited him outside for a whipping. Everyone's eyes opened wide and a few wise guys figured that this was where I was going to get licked. When I got him outside, I bribed him to scream and holler like he was getting whipped good. When we went back in, it was as quiet as death. But Lord, I had to pay him off every month. There was hardly enough left over for me."

Leonor giggled. Magdalena continued to stare at him, not cracking a smile. "Now that you've failed as a teacher," she said, "what do you do?"

"He works at the bank," Leonor said, coming to his defense.

Magdalena drew back, startled, and her eyes narrowed to slits. "What bank?" she said.

"Southwest Citizens."

"Grandfather's bank," Leonor said.

It had been tense and unreceptive before, but now the suspicion surged like the rushing Río Grande at flood time. "What do you do at the bank?" she asked.

Antonio was disturbed by this sudden, intense hostility. What is it? he thought. Why is she so angry? "Bookkeeping. And I sometimes help as a teller."

"And you snoop into people's accounts."

Antonio was stunned. His mouth fell open. "Oh, Auntie!" Leonor protested. "How could you?"

"No, señora," Antonio finally stammered. He looked in desperation at Leonor, as if asking what he had done wrong.

"It's just a temporary job until he goes to work for the government," Leonor said.

Magdalena turned her glowering slits of eyes at Antonio. She was breathing deeply, hurriedly, the only sign of agitation on her rigid, stonelike exterior.

"I passed the Civil Service examination," he said, "to be a railway mail clerk. To work on the trains. I'm waiting for an assignment. It's very secure. And you get to travel everywhere. Tucumcari, Gallup, El Paso. Even Phoenix and Los Angeles."

"That's your future?" Magdalena said sarcastically. "That's getting off the farm? A traveling man. Being a guard on a mail car?"

"It's very important," Antonio said. "You have to carry a revolver because of train robbers. You have to know all the post offices of all the towns on the route. Sometimes you have to stay awake all night in order to work the mail. It pays well, and you have a job for life."

But Magdalena had not been listening. Her suspicious eyes bored hard into his. "So you found out at the bank that Leonor's family is rich."

Leonor jumped to her feet and stomped from the room. The confused Antonio looked first at Magdalena, then to the departing Leonor, then back at Magdalena, shaking his head that he had done no such thing.

"I—I have to leave," he said stiffly, trying to control his temper as he hurried after Leonor.

11

Popular song

"C'llegiate, c'llegiate
Yes! we are collegiate
Nothing intemedjate,
No ma'am."

The little frame house on the outskirts of town was ablaze with lights. They glowed through window shades like candles glowing through the eyes of a jack-o'-lantern. The uncurbed dirt road was lined with roadsters, sedans, and rumble seat coupes parked up to the nearest edge of a neighbor's cornfield. Music muted by the closed windows and doors burst out in full strength as couples entered and left the house. Above the melodies of "Whispering while you cuddle near me," and "Yes, sir, that's my baby," hummed the excited hubbub of a party.

The cool night air was country dark except for the house and pinpoints of sparkling stars up high. A young man in the side yard held his stomach and leaned against a cottonwood tree retching. An indignant female voice nagged, "Donnie! You're disgusting! Take me home this very minute." Donnie retched again.

From the back of the house came the shout, "Pelea! Fight! Kelly's at it again!" Inside dancers bounced to the syncopated rhythms of, "No, sir, don't mean maybe. Yes, sir, that's my baby now."

Leonor, flushed with excitement, stood against the rolled up carpet on the edge of the living room, holding Antonio's hand. To their right a group of young women huddled around the Victrola.

"Oh, Billy's records are just swell," one of them squealed.

"Did you see his Atwater Kent? He promised to get the dance band at the Savoy Ballroom at midnight."

"Wait. Wait. I want to hear this record first. Billy—!"

Leonor had never been to such a party. For one thing, they were older and very, very sophisticated. Most of the girls smoked cigarettes, some of them posing with long ivory cigarette holders. The liquor flowed ceaselessly, and she allowed herself a few sips of Antonio's punch so they wouldn't think she was a goody-goody. Ugh! It was too strong, burning down to the pit of her stomach.

Emma Wheatley's headband had slipped down to her eyebrows. She pushed it up with a wobbly forefinger and turned dazedly toward their host who had danced by. "Billy. Who's your bootlegger? Marvelous. Just the cat's pajamas."

Billy Hammock grinned and hopped back into the middle of the crowded dance floor. "Gene Austin, Billy!" another girl screeched. "The new Gene Austin."

"Let's get some air," Antonio said. "It's too hot in here."

Leonor could barely take her eyes from the dancers as she tapped her foot in time to the music. It was a mixed crowd, almost equally divided between Spanish-Americans and Anglos. For the most part they were young people of the middle class, few if any of them rich. Likewise few were poor. The poorest was her cousin, Theresa, who made up for it by being the prettiest. The young men and women danced with one another unselfconsciously, the products of decades of cultural elbow-rubbing, familiar with each other's customs and language, dating and even marrying each other. If anyone had accused them of being tolerant, they would not have understood. Tolerant? What was there to be tolerant about? Except maybe bootlegging.

"Oh, this air feels good," Tony said as they pushed through the crowd onto the front porch. Leonor smiled. Tony looked so handsome, and he was dressed so stylishly. His hair was slicked back and his bright brown face glowed just like—like an Arab sheik's.

"I was afraid that your aunt wouldn't let you come," he said.

She smiled. She dared not tell the truth. Her aunt did not even know that she was out. Magdalena was at the café tonight, and Leonor had conspired with Lupe, who with her simple good heart rejoiced in romance and felt compassion for the girl who had so recently lost her grandfather. Ssh! Lupe had whispered. Don't worry. She'll never know. Have a good time. And tell me about it afterwards. About the pretty dresses and the food and the handsome boys.

"I don't think your aunt likes me," Tony said.

"She's only my aunt. My father will like you. And my mother would have too."

"My mother will love you," Tony said. "And my father—" His words trailed off hesitantly. "It's just—he doesn't understand why I don't want to milk cows the rest of my life. He's pretty old-fashioned."

The screen door slammed. "There you are," Theresa said. "How are you two doing?" Leonor and Tony looked away from each other in embarrassment. "They're going to turn on the radio after they play one more record."

The boisterous conversation in the house dropped to a buzz. Above the murmur of young voices came the strain of a single violin, followed by a piano. Then the casual tenor, homey as a best friend, simple as pure water, crooned the lyrics with a feeling as ineffable as the clear, bright stars twinkling down upon them.

> Just Mollie and me
> And Baby makes three
> We're happy in my
> Blue heaven.

The violin played a sweet solo. The crooner hummed a chorus as the piano tinkled in the background. Then the sounds of tenor and piano interwove while the violin sang in the background.

Three and a half minutes of romance and sentiment transformed from grooved disk to romantic tenor had reached to the heart of all that Leonor yearned for. Tony held her hand as the lyrics thrilled her with promises of the beautiful future unrolling before them.

As the song ended, Leonor turned in the dark, misty eyed and tingling. Then she heard the soft sniffling. Someone inside parted the curtains and the light fell across her cousin's face. Theresa was trying to hold back, but finally a cry burst from her lips and tears flooded her swollen red eyes. She rushed down the steps into the dark.

"Theresa!" Leonor called. She peered toward the road but the dark had swallowed her cousin. She rushed from the porch, searching left and right, until she saw a ghostlike shape. Theresa was leaning against the rumble seat of José's coupe, her face in her hands, sobbing uncontrollably.

"I lost my baby," Theresa cried. "God punished me for doing wrong. Oh, Leonor, don't ever do anything wrong!"

"Theresa!" José's voice was perplexed and irritable.

"What's the matter?" Tony asked.

The young men's footsteps crunched on the gravel road as they approached the coupe. José turned Theresa around and took her hands. His voice was strained with impatience and remorse. "Come on, honey. We'd better go home." Then he turned to Tony and whispered, "She's had too much to drink."

"My baby," Theresa whimpered.

A voice shouted from the house. "Hey! Come on. We've got the band at the Savoy."

"Let's go home!" José commanded.

Leonor and Tony stood in the dark watching as the taillights of the coupe, tiny as stars, faded down the dirt road towards town. It was, Leonor thought, the saddest thing she had ever seen. But why had José seemed almost angry? Couldn't he see how painful it was for Theresa?

Then Magdalena's angry face seemed to stare at her from the night. Leonor abruptly pulled her hand from Tony's. "It's midnight," she said. "I have to be home."

After wishing Billy Hammock a happy birthday again, they drove in silence to Old Town. Tony parked in the shadow of a cottonwood tree some distance from the house and walked her quietly to the back door. When he leaned to kiss her, Leonor turned away.

"No," she said. "Please."

He drew back and waited as she knocked. "Lupe," she called in a low voice. "Lupe, it's me."

12

Evening Journal

Proceedings in Probate Court: Petition to
sell certain property in the estate
of George E. Ellis was granted.

Santa Fe Is for Al Smith

It was unusually quiet during the morning shift at the Wigwam
Motor Court. There were very few telephone calls. When it was quiet
like this, Nicolás would sit in the little room next to the office, leaving
the door open so he could see anyone who came to the counter and
hear the telephone if it rang. He practiced softly on the Mexican
guitar he had bought years ago in Juárez, singing in an impassioned
tenor that lent itself to the tunes of the day. From time to time, when
his bar bills mounted and even the bartenders he knew refused him
credit, he would pay off his debts by performing.

Today, other possibilities were on his mind. Two of his cronies
who made marginal livings playing at weddings and dances had asked
him to join in an audition at the local radio station. One of them knew
the manager, and with the large Spanish-speaking population in the
area, songs in Spanish had a ready audience.

Nicolás had been working on a very popular song, "Mi viejo amor"
(An Old Love), singing to his own accompaniment, when the telephone rang. It was Alfonso Vigil who asked—no, commanded him, to
come to the office. It was important.

So after the audition Nicolás called on Vigil. He placed his guitar
case on the floor and watched apprehensively as Vigil gave instruc-
tions to his secretary. Perhaps Magdalena had changed her mind and
agreed to let him petition for an advance. Or perhaps Vigil had spoken

to her and explained that their father had agreed to lend Nicolás the money for the Wigwam.

Vigil sat impassively until the door closed. "I thought it best that we discuss this in person. I don't like telephones. They're almost as undependable as motor cars.

"It appears," Vigil said, "that your sister is contesting your father's will."

Nicolás was shocked. His lips flapped wordlessly in disbelief. He felt a surge of anger. He looked down at his long, slim, guitar-playing fingers curled for attack and wished that Magdalena was within reach.

"I . . . I don't understand," he stammered. "The bitch!"

The profanity bounced off the lawyer's cast-iron composure. He went on as if he hadn't heard. "She claims that Dionisio intended to change his will. He decided to leave everything to her, no strings attached. The fact that he had signed over the house was evidence of that, she says. It was for taking care of the old man the last few years of his life."

"Her housekeeper took care of him. And he paid her. But what about my loan?" Vigil shrugged. "And Leonor. What about Leonor?"

"Señora Soto claims that there were to be no strings attached. She claims she can leave her estate, including that which she inherits from your father, to whomever she wants."

"Does that mean Leonor gets nothing?"

"I have no idea of the terms of your sister's will—if she has one."

"But nothing from Father's estate?"

"That's what she claims."

Nicolás couldn't believe it. What had gotten into that thief? It was unfair. Had their father really told Magdalena that he was going to change his will? He doubted that. Dionisio doted on his granddaughter. He would never leave Leonor without a legacy.

Nicolás thrust his head forward angrily. "I'll fight it!" he said, hitting the arm of the chair with a clenched fist.

Vigil nodded serenely. "There are some legal technicalities."

"You mean you're to be her lawyer?"

He talked to Nicolás as if speaking to a not very bright small boy. "No. I'm your father's lawyer. I represent the estate. It would be a conflict of interest for me to represent her. It would also be a conflict of interest for me to represent you."

"You mean I have to get another lawyer?"

"No. Just that you might want to talk to one. I will still be involved, representing the estate. In that sense I will also represent you and your daughter, who are mentioned in the only will we are aware of. But you may want to consult another lawyer. There may be other aspects of this that will be impossible for me to handle. You understand?"

Nicolás nodded abruptly, even though he really did not understand. What he did understand was that another lawyer meant fees, money that he didn't have.

He rubbed his throbbing temples, glancing around the office in nervous exasperation. "What . . . what does it mean? I mean how do these things work? What can happen?"

"The courts honor duly executed wills. Your father handled all his legal affairs through me for years. We have his will that is being filed with the probate court."

"You mean that contesting the will is . . . is a sham?"

"I didn't mean to imply that. Wills are sometimes contested."

"But what happens?"

"Unless there is another later will, usually nothing. Except—"

Nicolás lifted his throbbing head expectantly. "Yes?"

"Except for delays. Sometimes quite long delays. And the added legal fees that come out of the estate."

"Jesus Christ!" There went any chance for an advance. There went any chance of buying half interest in the Wigwam. It had turned into another of those rancorous struggles with his sister that he had thought were over forever. Struggles like when growing up, with her reaching greedily for anything that was his, whether she really wanted it or not. Painful struggles like the one in which he had given up his daughter to another to raise. Struggles that were senseless and exasperating, as if she were trying to reduce him to nothing for no reason at all. Oh, why couldn't people just be nice to each other and go their happy ways?

"You see what it is!" Nicolás shouted, his frustration and anger finding voice. "She knows she can't overthrow the will. She just wants to spite me. To keep me from buying the Wigwam. To make me suffer. She's a malicious, crazy woman!"

The lawyer sat as impassive as ever, not betraying by the slightest expression or motion what it was he really thought. "I wanted to tell you in person," he said. "We'll go ahead with the probate court filing.

But you may want to consult another lawyer, so I thought it best to talk to you. Your sister is being represented by—" He mentioned the name of a local firm.

"Those shysters!" Nicolás spat.

"Unless you have any other questions—?"

Nicolás shook his head and stood, stumbling over his guitar case. He snatched it from the floor and made his way out of the office deep in thought and aggravation.

13

Morning Tribune

Uncle Sam Has a Big Surplus
for End of Midyear

Pick Albuquerque As Major Airport

From Alfonso Vigil's office on the second floor of the First National Bank Building, it was three blocks to Southwest Citizens Bank at Second Street and Gold Avenue.

A young man was closing the front door when Nicolás approached, a vaguely familiar young man who looked like a Rafa. Nicolás knocked quickly on the glass, mouthing his words exaggeratedly, as the attendant secured the lock.

"I have to come in. To see Ramón Springer." The young man peered at Nicolás and a look of recognition lit his face. "Ramón Springer," Nicolás repeated. "I have to see Señor Springer." The lock snapped back, and the door opened just enough for Nicolás to slip through. "Thank you," he said.

"You're welcome, Señor Armijo."

Nicolás was too intent on his mission to wonder how the young man knew his name. The cashiers behind the brass partitions on the marble counters were settling up the day's accounts. It would have been a relatively quiet day. Fridays were the busy ones. The bank was a block from the railroad station, a site selected by Nicolás's father many years ago, with easy access for workers on the trains and at the railroad maintenance shops, a string of giant buildings along First Street. Fridays were paydays, and the Spanish-speaking laborers patronized the bank that spoke their language.

A matronly woman stood beside Ramón's desk holding a stack of folders. Nicolás waited outside the door while Springer told her to verify the employment of a loan applicant. On the wall behind the desk hung a large, framed oval photograph of a young man in khaki, Ramón Springer in his 1918 doughboy's uniform. Beside the photograph hung the grim khaki gas mask with blind celluloid eyes staring out at Nicolás. While on the other side of the photograph a sheathed bayonet was mounted at an angle. A cane hung on a hat rack that stood behind the desk.

As soon as the woman left, Springer stood awkwardly, favoring his left leg. He smiled and tossed a quick military salute at Nicolás. "Well, come in. Close the door." He stretched across the wooden desk, hand extended.

"You haven't been to the Legion meetings lately," Ramón chided. "I heard you at the speak on First Street a few weeks ago." Ramón nodded toward the guitar case.

"The American Legion is for young fellows," Nicolás said. "Those who fought in France."

"But Cuba," Ramón said. "What about Cuba? That must have been a war. San Juan Hill. Riding behind Colonel Roosevelt. Did you think then that he would become President? I envy you, Nicolás."

Nicolás smiled sadly, looking askance at the cane and the gas mask, then at the eagerly smiling younger man. Ramón had been but a boy when they first met, back from two years of college in Illinois to help in the bank that his father, along with Dionisio Armijo and James Wheeler, had founded. Nicolás had worked in the bank then, had helped train the young man who was thirteen years his junior. Showing the young Ramón how to drink like a New Mexican. Filling him with stories of Cuba and the military so that in 1918, Springer could not wait to leave his childless young wife for the adventure and glory of war in Europe.

"Listen," Ramón said, "you should take that guitar of yours to the new moving picture palace. The owners are clients of ours. They still owe us for half of the theater."

"We auditioned for the radio," Nicolás said. "You have to think big."

Ramón smiled. "Well, did you come to buy me a drink after work like the old days? Or is there something I can do for you?"

Nicolás's heart did a flip-flop. His buoyant facade disappeared. He was uncomfortable asking favors of friends, uncomfortable that he would have to feign enthusiasm when what he felt was fear.

He leaned forward, speaking in a low, urgent voice. "I have a chance to buy Eddie Carr's half of the Wigwam. It's a great opportunity."

"How much is he asking?"

Nicolás told him. Ramón's eyebrows rose in disbelief. "Have you gone over the books?"

"No. I mean I've looked at them. But somehow I get confused when I look at numbers. Banking was never my business. Music I can read, but numbers fool me."

"Oh, Nicolás," Ramón said.

Nicolás's words came rapidly now, urgently, racing after but not quite catching the promise of help that he saw fleeing.

"It's a great opportunity. A chance. A great chance. I need to be in something that works for a change. Something new. Something with promise. I'm not a young man anymore, Ramón. Not a success like you. Look at you. Only thirty-five and already president of a bank. I need a loan! I want to make something of myself before it's too late."

The younger man looked away in embarrassment. "We've always had collateral from your father before—God rest his soul."

"There's my share of his estate—"

"Going through the courts. That could take months. We'd need a release from the courts."

"And—and what about the Wigwam itself? If I can't pay back the loan, the bank could take my half."

"It's overpriced, Nicolás. Carr is trying to rook you."

"But—but—"

"Do you need a small personal loan? A little something to tide you over until your inheritance comes through? We're old friends. I can do that much for an old friend."

"But the Wigwam—"

"I'm sorry, Nicolás. If you want, I'll look over the books. But you'll have to come up with a good down payment before the bank can lend you the rest. That's a lot of money."

"Oh, God, Ramón. Why does everything I touch turn out like this?"

The younger man rose, buttoning his suit coat. He reached to the hat rack for his cane and came around the edge of the desk, limping slightly. He put a hand on Nicolás's shoulder. "Come on," he said. "Let's go down to the club. I'll buy you a drink."

14

Evening Journal

George Remus, Bootleg King, Gets Freedom

Zuni Indians Ready for
Olympic Tryouts at University

On the first of each month Magdalena usually awoke glowing with anticipation. This was the day that she tallied the receipts from her restaurant. It was like letting gold and silver run through her hands, and she basked in the power that they gave her. Profits! More! Wonderful! she would whisper to herself. Then she would collect the rent from the tenant of the land left by her first husband. She crowned her day by triumphantly depositing her riches in the bank. Then she would go home exhilarated and exhausted, with a calm peacefulness, almost as if in the afterglow of making love.

This first of the month there was something extra to look forward to: the rents from the grazing land in the foothills and from the ten acres north of Old Town plaza. Although they were part of her father's estate, she already considered them hers. She had not heard from either of the tenants, but she knew them by name and by reputation, the way she knew many of the people in the sparsely populated rural areas.

Yet she opened her eyes with a sense of foreboding this morning, with the fear that her good fortune was not real. That something or someone was trying to take it from her. Before her father had died, she had reviled him for his slovenly senile ways, for eating and drinking too much, for his crotchety temper and cantankerous opposition to most of what she did. But after his death, being superstitious, Magdalena spoke nothing but his praises. She sensed vaguely, without being able to put it into words, that if she did not praise him, he would come back to haunt her—bringing with him all those many dead whom he had joined and who vastly outnumbered the living.

This morning, her new sources of income reminded her of her father. She tried to remember what it was she had dreamed, knowing only that she had ground her teeth until they were ready to snap and had awakened in the middle of the night trembling with fear.

"It's nothing," she admonished herself. "Just nerves."

She bustled into the kitchen in her usual officious way. "Lupe. These eggs are cold. Fry me two more."

Lupe turned from the wood stove, her brown face shiny from the heat. "I just took them out of the frying pan," she said.

Magdalena turned in her chair and glared. "Fry me two more eggs, Lupe!"

"If you'd eat them right away instead of complaining, they'd be hot enough. It's a sin to waste food."

Magdalena's eyes narrowed. Stubborn Indian, she said to herself. "You didn't pick up around the house yesterday. The newspaper is still on the living room floor."

Lupe set the coffeepot on the stove and lumbered out of the kitchen. She stormed back with a folded newspaper, opened a stove lid with a metal handle, and thrust the paper into the fire. She watched it flare into yellow flames and crumbling cinders before dropping the lid over the opening.

"Fry me two more eggs!" Lupe crossed her arms and stood stubbornly immobile. "Are you going to force me to fire you again?"

As Lupe untied her apron, Leonor shuffled into the kitchen yawning. She stopped and laid a newspaper on the table. Lupe hung her apron on a door peg and glared at Magdalena. "Juan and I are leaving. There are plenty more jobs around. Better jobs."

"You haven't fixed my breakfast," Leonor said.

"Let *her* fix it," came the answer as Lupe left. "She's the only one who knows whether or not an egg is hot."

"Oh, Auntie," Leonor said. "What are you two fighting about this time?"

"Lupe!" Magdalena shouted. "Juan has to drive me on my collections this morning! You know I can't drive." A door slammed, then silence.

"Auntie, it will be a week before you get them back."

"I'll just drive myself," Magdalena said testily. "There's nothing to driving." She picked at her eggs, then crumpled the newspaper and threw it at the stove. "This is yesterday's. That dumb Indian burned today's."

Leonor went to the stove and slid a frying pan over the heat. The back door slammed again, and a heavy tread came up the hall. "All right," Lupe said. "Get away from my stove." Leonor sat at the table. "If it wasn't for you," Lupe said to her, "I'd have left this crazy house for good."

"Is the car ready?" Magdalena demanded.

"Why don't you ask Juan. He's your driver."

Magdalena left her eggs which now were cold, eating the potatoes fried with green chili. She stood abruptly and headed for the back door. That woman will be the death of me, she thought. "Juan! I'm leaving in ten minutes!"

"Sí, señora."

She sat in the back seat, cursing the stubborn and irritable Lupe. The tenor of the day had been set. The little adobe house of her first tenant stood mutely unresponsive to her knock, although she swore she could hear rustling inside.

She ordered Juan to guard the back of the house while she stood at the front door, pounding impatiently. "Look in the windows!" she shouted. Then a child's voice babbled in Spanish, and she knew that she had flushed them out.

The man of the house, a distant cousin of the prominent Salazars, peered through the sliver of opening in the front door, his hangdog face bleary-eyed. They had been asleep, he claimed. Begging your pardon, patrona, but it was the truth as God was his witness. He meant no disrespect. It was just so early in the morning.

Magdalena looked at the watch pinned to the lapel of her coat. Nine o'clock. Late enough for anyone to be up, especially a farmer. He bowed in deference as she glared at him.

It was a bad time, the tenant continued. It was always a bad time, she countered—for her too. Things were not so good, he said. His family had barely enough to eat, and the baby was sick. The water table was rising—the river was extra full this year—and there was less dry land on which to grow corn and beans.

The rent is due today, she repeated. He had been her tenant for years. He knew what day it was. Or did he want her to send him a calendar free of charge?

He had been working at the sawmill—when there was work. There had only been enough work for the regulars lately. Just a few more days, señora. He was certain that he could pay her then.

She slowly shook her head and extended her hand. She did not believe him. He was trying to gyp her—to cheat her of what was rightfully hers. In a moment his wife would come to the door on cue, holding under one arm a snot-nosed baby that was wearing a smelly rag for a diaper and who would begin to whimper.

"All we have is what we owe the doctor," he said.

She continued to shake her head, her hand extended. The tenant disappeared into the house and returned with a handful of grubby bills and dirty coins.

"I'll have to sell one of my goats," he said. But her hand remained extended as he counted out the month's meager rent. She watched every bill and coin as they dropped reluctantly into her hand. You can't trust anybody, she thought. If you're not rooking them, they're trying to rook you.

Next Magdalena ordered Juan to drive to Alameda, a squat little village north of Albuquerque, to call on the rancher who leased the grazing land from her father. She wondered what excuse she would hear this time.

A plump pigeon of a woman with an anxious smile answered the door. Señor Peralta had ridden to Bernalillo, his wife said. As Magdalena's disbelieving and suspicious eyes searched the inside of the house, Señora Peralta quickly added that he would be back soon. Then she expressed her condolences over Dionisio's death. El patrón, she called him. Such a fine man.

The señora led Magdalena into the sala and served her a cup of lukewarm, bitter coffee—yesterday's coffee. Then Señora Peralta sat across from Magdalena, repeating her condolences and reciting her own litany of sorrows, past and present.

No, Peralta said when he returned. There was no monthly payment. He and Señor Armijo had arranged for the lease to be paid yearly when he received the money from his flocks. But he could not find the paper that he and Dionisio had signed, and Magdalena's face hardened. Another one, she said to herself. They're all the same.

"Well, no matter," the rancher said. "Señor Armijo and I always settled business with a handshake. The paper was just for the lawyers who never believe anything unless it's signed in blood."

Finally, his pigeon of a wife fluttered into the room waving the paper as if it were the long lost deed to half the state of New Mexico. Magdalena read it warily. Yes, that looked like her father's signature. But could she be sure?

It was then that Peralta asked if she wanted to sell the land. It was desert, he said. Far east of the city. Not good for much besides sheep and jackrabbits. But he was a sheepman, and so it had some value to him.

She looked around the neat, clean interior of the little adobe house, furnished comfortably but without much taste. The rancher and his wife looked like many others of their kind.

"I could give you a down payment," he said. His eyes lit up shrewdly. He could almost hear the clink of silver dropping into the cash box that she used for a brain. "In cash. We could settle the rest when the courts do whatever they have to do to your father's estate."

It was too tempting. When the rancher brought out a strongbox and started counting the green bills, Magdalena didn't even argue the price. She could already feel the crisp comfort of money. The impropriety of the transaction without court approval or her brother's agreement never entered her mind. The land was hers to do with what she wished. The green of money was more important than any number of acres of scrubby desert.

Magdalena walked from the house smugly comforted by the bills tucked in her purse alongside her copy of the scrawled agreement. She did not tell Juan about her good stroke of business. She ordered him to drive to the bank immediately because she felt uneasy carrying so much cash.

After lunch she reviewed receipts with the cashier at the café. Then Juan drove her to the ten acres left by her father.

"Stop here!" she cried some distance from the house.

She stepped cautiously from the sedan and walked along the border of the property, studying it carefully. Unlike the smaller property north and nearer to the river, and unlike the grazing land miles east at the foot of the Sandía Mountains, this ten acres appealed to her. She could see the possibilities in it. Not for farming, although it was good farm land, far enough from and high enough above the river. The high water table that infected much of the rich land along the

Río Grande was not a problem here. But it would be a waste to use this land for farming. The city was growing. Old Town and New Town were merging, and these ten acres were right in the middle. Land that could be developed and subdivided into lots. Land on which houses could be built and sold for a tidy profit. Land on which one could make a small fortune. Ten acres and such-and-such numbers of lots per acre. Think of the possibilities!

Juan followed slowly in the sedan. Far off, in the middle of the field, a man rose and turned, leaning on a hoe, staring at her with suspicion. Well, Magdalena thought. My new tenant. I wonder what his excuse will be.

15

Morning Tribune

High School Senior Class of 163 to Graduate June 1

Many Political Allusions in Papal Encyclical; Expresses Regret at Women Wearing Less

Leonor had recently volunteered to help in the café after school. She wanted to earn some money of her own for—she was not sure. For an emergency. Or for something special. Though in truth it was also a bribe to heaven so that her aunt would continue to spend Friday and Saturday nights at work.

Magdalena was pleased at her niece's apparent sense of duty. But she was more pleased with Leonor's willingness to work than she was with her niece's desire to be paid. Why, Magdalena responded, you should pay me! Everything that you have comes from me! But Leonor was not deceived. She knew that her father sent monthly checks for her keep.

As if heaven had responded, Magdalena started to stay late on Thursday and Sunday nights also. It freed Leonor's evenings from her aunt's suspicious eyes. And Lupe tolerated if not encouraged Leonor to see Antonio.

This afternoon Leonor dropped her schoolbooks on the usual corner table. The waitress smiled and offered her a soda, but Leonor wanted to do her work and hurry home.

Magdalena greeted her, glowing with self-satisfaction. Her usually tight face was relaxed. Even Magdalena's eyes were properly focused. She spoke in Spanish, her deep voice lisping the Castilian that she affected as the speech of the upper classes, at once proper and a sign of education. Unlike the gutter Spanish spoken by the local riffraff.

"What do you think happened today?" she asked. Her mouth protruded in a tight smile.

It was the opening gambit in a game, and it depressed Leonor. With that grim smile and softened demeanor, it could only mean that Auntie had triumphed over someone. It reminded her of an insect she had read about in biology. Was it the praying mantis? Where the female enticed the male to fertilize her eggs. Then, when he had served his purpose, she killed and devoured him—sometimes while still in the very act of fertilization. But did praying mantises gloat?

"It was something nice." Leonor's voice was flat. Bored.

The tight smile broadened. "Very."

Well, it had something to do with money, Leonor thought. "I don't know, Auntie."

"You're not trying," her aunt chided playfully. Leonor did not want to play. If Auntie wanted to gloat, let her gloat. Out with it! "I'll give you a hint. It's something that every woman who wants to be her own person should do."

"Make money," Leonor said.

The disappointment on Magdalena's face was immediate. She stared with her grim, tight, normal expression. "Don't be smart!"

"Well, it is, isn't it? Isn't that what you wanted me to guess? You made a lot of money today."

"Why do you say it that way? As if . . . it were wrong?"

"I didn't say it any way. All I said was that you made a lot of money today. You're just mad because I guessed."

"The cook needs you in the kitchen," Magdalena said. But Leonor knew that it was not over. Before she left it would come up again. But she didn't care. She had answered her aunt honestly. What did the woman want?

Leonor's improper response did not escape the cashier's notice. "You're such a smart businesswoman, patrona," she fawned. "I wish I were half as smart as you."

Magdalena's pleased and laughing denial encouraged the cashier. The cook looked at Leonor and blew a silent kiss at the air, nodding at the cashier's falsely saccharine words. "She steals from the cash register," the cook whispered. "I know, but I can't prove it. She's very clever."

It takes a thief to fool a thief, Leonor thought. And she worked in a fury, impatient to be done and away.

"Bye, honey," the cook said when Leonor was finished. "You're such a good worker."

Leonor gathered her schoolbooks and approached her aunt's table. "Sit down," Magdalena ordered. "I want to talk to you." She turned and glared at the waitress and the cook, both of whom retreated into the kitchen.

"I want to warn you about that young man."

"What young man?" Leonor asked.

"That won't do," Magdalena said. "I know. I know everything. All I have to do is ask Lupe." Leonor did not respond, unwilling to be tricked into an admission. She knew that Lupe would never betray her.

"He's just like all the rest," Magdalena said. "He's just after your money."

"What money?"

"He knows you're my niece and that I'm a shrewd businesswoman with properties of my own. He knows that your grandfather left everything to me. He works at the bank. He must know."

In many ways Leonor felt that she knew Antonio better than she knew her aunt. Didn't he telephone almost every night? Hadn't they been together as often as possible—to the movies at the new KiMo theater, to a party or a dance, for drives in his little coupe? No, she thought. Antonio was not like that at all. He was virtuous and pure. He was even upset when he learned that Leonor sneaked out of the house. He wanted her to have Magdalena's permission. And he had plans of his own, ambitions of his own. He was waiting impatiently for his appointment to the Railway Mail Service.

"We can move to California," he told her excitedly. "To L.A. We don't have to stay in this backward place all of our lives. We're young! We have things to do! Oh, Leonor, I love you so. It will be so wonderful!"

"That boy is a snoop. A fortune hunter," Magdalena said.

But her aunt's paranoia did not infect Leonor. She knew the truth. "No, Auntie," she said simply.

Leonor was determined not to discuss Antonio. She would see whomever she pleased and keep it to herself. It was her business. After all, she was an adult. Almost a high school graduate. She was old enough to get married if she wanted to. There were girls younger than she who already were married, who already had children.

Magdalena tried another tack. The cashier smiled at her from behind the cash register, and she was reminded once again of what she had started to tell Leonor earlier.

"This has been a wonderful day," Magdalena said. "I had an offer for that good-for-nothing desert near the Sandías that belonged to your grandfather. The rancher gave me a down payment. He didn't even argue about price. You see, you can beat them at their own game if you're shrewd."

"That's nice, Auntie."

Magdalena set her large, strong hand on her niece's small one. "You have a wonderful future ahead of you," she said. "Your aunt is rich. If you're a good girl and do the right things, Auntie will leave it all to you. You'll be an heiress. But being an heiress is not easy. You have to be careful. Especially of men. I know. I want you to listen and learn from someone who knows best."

Being an heiress meant little to Leonor. Not that she was cavalier about money. It was just that she did not know what it meant to be an heiress. Hadn't she been comfortable all her life? There was seldom anything she wanted that she did not get. Her father sent money every month. It must be enough because Auntie, who was somewhat of a miser, did not deny her much. Or was it that Leonor's wants were so few?

Then, she thought, what about Father? Didn't Grandfather leave him anything? While she could see that her aunt might have deserved more—after all, she had taken care of Grandfather these past few years—it did not seem fair that Father should be left out altogether.

Magdalena patted her hand. "You are the closest person in all the world to me. There is no one closer." But Leonor thought of her father, Auntie's brother and blood of her blood, and did not understand.

"There's nothing more in the world I want than for you to have all the things I didn't have as a girl. To feel secure and not have to worry about the rent or a pretty dress. To know that no matter what, everything will be all right because you have enough to make it all right. To be independent of everyone."

Her aunt's intense, dark eyes softened. It had never occurred to Leonor before, but she realized that there was no one in the world

close to her aunt. Her friends, if you could call them that, were either
servants, tenants, or employees. The friendships that Magdalena had
had over the years did not seem to last. They went through short,
intense periods that suddenly erupted into anger and separation.
Through the years, friendship was one thing that did not last. It was
fleeting, seasonal, falling like leaves in autumn to be replaced by new
leaves the following spring. But now the tree was barren and did not
renew itself.

Leonor's heart softened. She felt sorry for this old woman. How
terrible to go through life like that. What if she, Leonor, did not have
Antonio? Did not have her father? Did not have any of her friends?

"Oh, Auntie," she said, feeling Magdalena's loneliness with terrible anguish. "Why didn't you ever marry again?"

For an instant, caught off guard, Magdalena's eyes mirrored the
terrible fear that was a constant part of her. The pain was raw,
undisguised, a pleading for help. Then it disappeared as if a steel door
had slammed shut.

"What do you mean?" she said icily. "What have you heard?
What have people been saying? Whatever it is, it's not true. In the
eyes of the Church, I've only been married once. Those others don't
count."

Magdalena's eyes were strained, moving restlessly back and forth,
not daring to meet Leonor's gaze, afraid that her niece would see the
truth in them. The cashier suddenly stopped leaning against the cash
register and hurried into the kitchen.

"What has someone told you?" Magdalena insisted, her voice
rising.

"Nothing, Auntie."

"Then why did you say that? I don't believe you."

Leonor looked toward the door, wishing that she was hurrying
through the plaza toward home. The sympathy she had felt a moment
ago had turned to irritation. You couldn't say anything without being
misunderstood.

"Was it your father?" Magdalena persisted. "That boy at the
bank? It had to be one of them."

Leonor grabbed her schoolbooks and left the table. "Tell me!"
Magdalena shouted after her. "It was your father, wasn't it? That's
just his kind of underhanded trick. Well, don't believe him. He's—"

Leonor let the door slam behind her and ran, tears in her eyes, not wanting to hear what her aunt had to say. When she reached home, sweaty and irritable, the telephone rang. Lupe was nowhere in sight so she picked up the receiver.

"Hello," she said, trying to hold back the emotion in her voice.

Silence. A long, dead silence. "Hello?" The receiver on the other end of the line clicked dead.

16

Evening Journal

Prohi Agents Arrest Many over Weekend

Station WRVA Richmond
7:15 Central Standard Time
Negro Chorus of 1,000 Voices

There was never a sign on the outside of El Lugar. It had acquired the formality of its name over the years because owners changed frequently. When González's place soon became Peña's, then Leyva's and Padilla's in quick succession, there was no point in referring to it by the name of the owner. When someone said they were going to El Lugar, everyone knew what they meant.

It lay hidden off a dark country road under a cluster of cotton-wood trees in the center of the farming community of Los Rafas. The building was originally a one-room adobe country store that grew to a somewhat larger general store, but El Lugar did not refer to the store proper. It meant the one-time storage room, dance hall, room for rent that was part of the larger building but with a separate entrance.

Before 1920, when Prohibition became the law of the land, it had been a popular cantina serving local farmers and laborers. It had also been the meeting place for political rallies, but 1920 had been a watershed year for that too, with Women's Suffrage changing the nature of such rallies even in this slow-to-change community.

Now it was the local speakeasy, much too elegant a word for the dingy, dark, adobe cave where the current owner served a small selection of crude rotgut. Even women frequented the place. Not just women of easy virtue looking for a good time or a little money (preferably both), but hard-bitten farm women who insisted on accompanying their husbands to what once had been an exclusively male hangout.

The owner tried to add a little class to match its changing nature, hanging a serape on the wall that was invisible in the dark, sacrificing the income from a few tables in the center of the room to create a small dance floor, and hiring musicians on weekends.

Because El Lugar was small and poor and could not afford to pay for protection, it suffered more than its share of raids by Prohibition agents anxious to gain headlines and reputations for fighting crime. In between raids, local sheriff's deputies dropped in for drinks as part of the regular crowd.

Late one Friday night the trio of musicians had finished their last set and were putting away their instruments. Nicolás Armijo carefully snapped shut his guitar case, weary and not looking forward to the drive home. He was the one with a car, such as it was, who would drop off the others on his way. The other musicians had joined friends, eyed the unattached women at the table, and ordered a round of drinks. At this rate, Nicolás thought, we'll be lucky to break even for the night.

He stood at the edge of the dance floor, staring at the table, torn between joining them and heading immediately for home. As he picked up his guitar case, a voice called from the dark.

"Armijo! Hey, Cuñado. I have to talk to you."

He turned with a sinking feeling, not anxious to talk to anyone. He squinted, peering into the dark, and saw the short, stocky, mustachioed man approach smiling. It was one of his long lost brothers-in-law, Pedro Trujillo, whom he had not seen in months. Trujillo, unlike Nicolás's dead wife, was a crafty, not very bright man who made his way by intimidation and occasional petty larcenies which more than once lost him his job, but as yet had not landed him in jail.

Trujillo stood almost chest to stomach against the taller Nicolás and whispered without looking up. "It's too crowded in here. Let's go outside."

Nicolás signaled to the bass guitarist as he grasped his guitar case which he dared not leave because he knew he would never see it again if he did. He eased into the cool night air and country quiet in relief.

"Over there," Nicolás said, pointing toward his car. He slid onto the driver's seat and rolled down a window, carefully placing his guitar in the back seat before offering Pedro a cigarette.

Trujillo was no longer smiling. Nicolás saw the wary eyes studying him in the glow of the cigarette tips. "Hey, I read about your old man in the newspaper. Qué lástima."

Nicolas shrugged. "He was seventy-one years old."

"But to go like that. He might have lived ten more years."

"¿Quién sabe?"

Trujillo leaned across the seat, breathing his smoke-filled breath into Nicolás's face. "He must have been rich, your old man." Nicolás turned away, as much from the look of greed and the tactless comment as from the foul breath, and grunted. What the hell business was it of Trujillo's? Was he trying to set him up for a touch?

"No offense, Nicolás." Trujillo's voice was suddenly a little desperate, sensing that he had said something wrong—he didn't know exactly what. "It's not like he fell in the shithouse and drowned. I mean it was the acequia. People drown in ditches and rivers all—"

The lights from El Lugar winked at them as customers stumbled out the door. Nicolás drowned the sound of Trujillo's stupid chatter by mentally picking the chords of a popular song on his guitar.

"I mean we're relatives. Brothers-in-law. Even if Mariana has been dead for fifteen—"

Nicolás reached for the door handle. He didn't have to listen to this idiot, didn't even have to be polite. What the hell was the crazy fool driving at?

As if he sensed Nicolás's thoughts, Trujillo put a hand on his arm. "Listen," he said. "We got a chance to make some money. Big money."

Big money and Pedro Trujillo? Trujillo and big money didn't talk the same language, and he was incapable of learning it.

"You want us to play for a wedding," Nicolás said sarcastically.

Pedro's laugh was too loud. "That's what I always liked about you, Nicolás, your sense of humor. You're one funny guy."

Nicolás did not feel funny. "What's this about money?"

"I mean *big* money. Maybe thousands."

Nicolás looked away in disbelief. Just a few days ago he had all but gone down on his knees to Ramón Springer for money. Springer had finally approved a personal loan for old times' sake, but it wasn't nearly enough to buy the Wigwam. Now this wretched fool was talking to him about thousands.

Nicolás let go of the door handle and sat back. "Listen," Trujillo

said. "Your sister, she still has that café in Old Town, doesn't she?"
Nicolás started to tense again. "I hear she does good business. Real
good business. And I don't mean in tamales and enchiladas." Pedro
grinned knowingly. "It's after the kitchen closes that she makes her
real money. I hear she's got a real classy operation there. Good booze.
Even some of that Canadian whiskey."

"You'd have to talk to her about that," Nicolás said.

"She won't talk to me. You know her. Begging your pardon, but
she's one hard lady."

"I don't know anything about her business. Tamales, enchiladas,
or booze." Although he knew that Magdalena had converted her
daytime café into an after-hours place that was very popular with the
local Spanish Americans.

"What I mean is, if someone—you, for instance—could get hold
of some genuine, real quality liquor, she might take some of it off your
hands." Nicolás looked at him coldly. What kind of nonsense was this?
"No," Pedro pleaded. "I'm serious. Real good quality stuff. Come by
boat from Cuba to Matamoros, then upriver to Juárez. I mean really
good stuff."

"Why would anybody in his right mind ship good liquor from
Cuba to Matamoros? There's New Orleans. There's Corpus Christi.
For Christ's sakes, there's Miami."

"It was a mistake. They were headed for New Orleans, but the
federales were patrolling the coast as thick as mosquitos. So they
headed for Corpus, but the same damn thing. Plus those chingado
Texas Rangers. So New Orleans's and Corpus Christi's bad luck was
Matamoros's good luck."

"And you want me to ask my sister if she wants to take some of it
off your hands?"

"No. You don't understand." Trujillo slid across the seat and
pressed up against Nicolás. His voice lowered to a whisper, although
there was no one within a hundred feet.

"Look," Trujillo said, "I don't mean any of that penny ante stuff.
There's your sister's place, sure. But there are others too. I mean, your
trio plays around town. You know all the people. Lots of them. And I
know people where I've worked as a waiter. We know who we can
trust and who has the money to buy. I mean cash on delivery. Cash.
You see? I know where the stuff is, and we both know how to get
rid of it."

Why does he need me? Nicolás thought. "You mean that's all there is to it?"

Trujillo cleared his throat and reached for another cigarette. "Well, there is one more thing."

There always was, Nicolás thought.

"Capital." Ah, Nicolás thought.

"Not that much," Trujillo said quickly, reaching for Nicolás's arm to hold him back. "I figured with your father and all— Well. You're the perfect business partner."

Nicolás took a drag from his cigarette and blew smoke slowly out the car window. His scruples about liquor were minor. The Volstead Act was stupid. Signs of its stupidity were everywhere. Christ! Even little old ladies made wine in their laundry tubs. Bootlegging just filled an existing need. If the need wasn't there, bootleggers wouldn't exist.

But there was a lot to think about. The law, for one. He was afraid of the law, afraid of being caught and sent to prison. He was even more afraid of entrenched bootleggers. Whose territory would they be intruding on? Would there be reprisals? Who was going to run the stuff up from Juárez? No, sir. This was not for him.

But the thought of a quick, easy profit was intriguing. Thousands, Trujillo had said. His share as financier would be considerable. Maybe enough to buy the Wigwam outright.

Nicolás took another drag from his cigarette. "How much?" he asked.

Pedro told him. He had some of it already, and he was certain he could raise the rest. "Is that for the whole shipload?" Nicolás asked.

"No! Are you crazy? That's just for a share. There'll be other shares going to San Antonio and El Paso and other places. But our share will be enough. It's a big ship."

"When do you need the money?"

"By the end of the week."

The door to El Lugar swung open again. A man with a guitar case stood at the threshold in the dim light. "Armijo!" he shouted. Then a second man stepped out. "Compadre!" came the shout.

Nicolás blinked his headlights, and the men lurched toward them. "Listen," Nicolás said. "I still have some questions."

Trujillo squirmed impatiently, his voice filled with desperation. "What about the money? What do you think?"

"We need to talk some more."

"I gotta fish or cut bait. I gotta let them know by the end of the week."

"Where can we meet tomorrow?"

"The little chapel in Martínez Town. Nobody goes there during the day. It's more private than a bar."

"Eleven o'clock," Nicolás said. "I have to be at work by twelve."

Trujillo slid from the seat and slipped into the dark as the other members of the trio approached. "Who was that?" the bass guitarist asked.

"Hey, Nicky," the other musician said. "Let's get out of this dump. I wanna go home and get some sleep."

17

Morning Tribune

Midsummer Clearance Sale of Women's Hats $2.00

Tunney to Receive $400,000
for Title Bout in Chicago

Leonor noticed that Magdalena was more nervous and irritable than usual. Some nights the girl could hear her aunt pacing through the house as if searching for the sleep that eluded her. At other times the house was unnaturally still and silent, and she could imagine Magdalena tossing in bed, alternating between sleep and wakefulness.

Suddenly her aunt would find herself wide awake, listening to the silence. Something was wrong. It was too still. Something was going to happen. Something horrible. Magdalena could feel it pressing in on her in the dark. An invisible wave like the sudden shift of atmospheric pressure when the weather changed.

She looked toward the clock which ticked like a booming bass drum, like the beating of her heart magnified a thousandfold. She raised her head from the pillow and peered at the dim hands crawling slowly across its face. 1:30. My God! Had she been in bed so short a time? She rolled over for a closer look. As she stared, the large hand slipped imperceptibly to 1:31.

I'll let someone else answer this time, she said to herself. I'll let Lupe answer.

But Lupe had not stayed that night. She seldom did unless Magdalena or Leonor was sick. There was no one in the house to protect her. No one to shut off the piercing ring that assaulted her every nerve, that turned her blood to ice, that brought back the childhood terror of lying awake in the dark while evil things hovered about, reaching for her.

Yes, Leonor was there. But like all inconsiderate children, her niece could sleep through fire, flood, and earthquake.

Lord save me, she thought, crossing herself. I should have asked Leonor to sleep with me tonight.

But it was not only tonight. It had been last night. And the night before. What about tomorrow? And the night after that? And the night after that? God, how long would it go on? How was she going to bear it?

She lay on her back, stiff, tense, bathed in her own perspiration although it was a cold night and the fire in the potbellied wood stove had long since died.

Suddenly she was a child again. Poor little Magdalena. In the loft in the barn, hands clasped in fright, watching her cousin Luis stalking mice in the alfalfa. His eyebrows were lifted in a devilish inverted V. His eyes were narrow and cruel, and his smile evil, as catlike he approached the squeaking nest of baby mice. Then he pounced, suddenly rising with his prey in his hand, crossed the loft in a rush, and thrust the baby mouse down the neck of her dress. She screamed, rushing terror-stricken off the edge of the loft to the ground, bruising her leg but not feeling it, rushing in terror, screaming, "Papá! Papá!"

Had it been then or another time that merged into this memory of terror? Instead of Papá there had been her brother, coarse, dirty string in hand, whirling it like a lariat, the half-dead grasshopper weighting the end.

She ran, feeling the tiny mouse crawling down her chest, down her stomach, down her thigh. Afraid to slap it. Afraid that she might smash it, leaving the bloody pulp smeared against her flesh. And now this, the green slingshot, whirling round and round, ready to get her.

Oh, God! Those vile, crawly creatures. The embodiment of those invisible evils that crept and crawled through her dreams, leaving a slimy trail of fear. The unspeakable night monsters that stalked her.

Then the ring, piercing the faint tick of the clock that had settled back to normal. Then again. More terrifying than baby mice. Worse than green slingshots.

She turned and buried her head under the pillow, but it continued. Insistent! Compelling! What if it was an emergency this time? she thought. What if someone was calling? Someone who needed help. What if something important had happened? Events did not respect the clock. Events did not tell time or care to.

But she remained paralyzed, the pillow over her head, unable to blot out the ringing telephone. Three, four times. Then again. Until she gritted her teeth, shuddered, and rushed to the hall.

"Hello," Her voice was the rough, frightened whisper of someone roused from deep sleep. Silence. The static crackle of the telephone line. "Hello?"

"Hija," the hoarse, ghostly voice said. "Hija. It's me. It's Papá." Terror-stricken, her hand froze to the receiver although every nerve in her body screamed: Hang up! "Hija. I know what you're doing. I know. They won't let me rest until I come back to tell you."

Oh, God! she thought. It's *him* again. Not as a cockroach this time, crawling on the kitchen floor, but a voice over this wicked machine.

She was unable to talk, unable to cry, unable to let go of the telephone, barely able to hear the hoarse, ghostly voice. "I know, hija. I know."

She slumped to the floor, overcome, her last recollection that of the ghostly voice rasping, "It will never do. I can't rest until it's set right."

When she regained consciousness, the telephone receiver hung dangling above the floor, buzzing its flat, dead tone. She replaced it and dragged herself the endless distance to bed.

It was a nightmare, she told herself. The telephone never really rang. There was no one—*no thing*—there. It was all a dream.

Slipping under the blankets did not still her trembling. Her mind whirled in rapid agitation. It's Manuel, she thought, reaching back in memory to her second husband. He read about Papá's death, and now he wants to get even. Wants to claim the money he thinks I owe him. The bastard!

But that had been twenty years ago. Could anyone stay bitter that long? Bear a grudge that long? Come back after all that time to avenge himself? She would not know him if she saw him on the street. Twenty years was a lifetime ago. The handsome, husky, mustachioed gambler—sporting men they called them then—was now an old man. No doubt gray of hair. Thick through the middle. His face bloated by drink and dissipation. A high liver without a penny who was probably still going through the old motions like a mechanical doll, living off some woman. Only age had a way of taking one's charm, one's looks, and living became harder, more desperate.

Yes, she remembered. He had been the one who had tried to beat her, the son-of-a-bitch. Until she finally took the revolver, that same weapon with which her first husband had blasted a hole in his temple, and threatened Manuel if he dared touch her again. She had gotten the best of him too, stopping payment on the check with which she had bribed him to get an annulment and to leave town.

From her fears and her memories, she conjured the handsome Manuel Castillo, fleetingly seeing his seductive smile, the charm with which lies flowed from his kissable lips, the smooth feel of his strong fingers big as sausages. He was floating over the foot of her bed, smiling invitingly, and she shuddered, confused by his seductive appeal coupled with his talent for betrayal.

He would not let her alone, not even when another figure conjured from fear and memory joined him. The serious Gabriel Soto, her third husband, who watched her shrewdly as if he knew where it would all end. Yes, she thought. The words over the telephone were too perceptive, too intelligent for Manuel. They were more like the words Gabriel would use. Gabriel, cheated of his cantina, which was the ultimate justice since it had been Gabriel who had cheated in marriage, taking her as his bride while he had another wife. Yes, she thought. Gabriel.

Even that image did not remain fixed, for soon she heard the giant squeak of a cockroach, and she knew that Papá was back. It *was* Papá. Papá's ghost. The countryside was full of ghosts. All one had to do was whisper, and someone would step forward to tell about visions in a cornfield at midnight. The dead never stayed dead. They prowled the earth restlessly, searching for that which they had never found in life.

"R-i-i-i-ng!" The shrill scream hit her like a blow.

I'll let it ring this time, she thought. I won't answer. She buried herself deep under the blankets, pulling them over her head, trembling so violently that she could barely keep herself covered.

"R-i-i-i-ng!"

A soft patter of footsteps down the hall. Then a soft whisper that she could not understand. It could have been the wind, a sigh, a moan.

"Auntie."

Magdalena screamed, turning her terrified eyes toward the voice, raising her head above the corners, expecting to see a bruja, a witch, a ghost. Then the white figure came at her, reaching out as she closed her eyes, and she felt a hand on her shoulder.

"Auntie, are you all right?"

"A ghost," she gasped. "A ghost."

"Auntie." The bed sagged. "It's all right, Auntie. You had a nightmare."

She looked up in terror. The circles under her eyes had grown darker, like eyes that had stared restlessly through many sleepless nights.

"When I answered, they hung up," Leonor said. "It must have been a wrong number."

"No," Magdalena said, shaking her head.

Leonor yawned and stood. "Don't go," Magdalena pleaded. "Stay with me. It's cold."

18

Evening Journal

Will Rogers Gives John D. Rockefeller a Dime

All Cities to Have Air Mail in Ten Years

"Mrs. Soto," Lawyer Florencio Apodaca protested. "Magdalena." The slim, dark little man sat behind the huge desk, dwarfed by it and by his client who sat across from him. His jet black hair was slicked back in the style of the day, wafting perfumed brilliantine throughout the office. He twitched his upper lip, the thin mustache exaggerating the motion.

"But he gave me cash," she insisted. "It's already in the bank."

Apodaca picked up the agreement and admonished her by shaking it like a warning forefinger. "My dear," he said. "You cannot enter into this unless your brother agrees and the court approves. It's a matter of law."

Magdalena's face clouded angrily. "I don't want to hear that," she said. "I'm the administrator of the estate. My father promised to leave everything to me. That's why I hired you. To prove that. And since it's all mine, I can do anything I want with it."

"No, no, dear lady. There is the law. Until the estate comes out of probate, you need court approval and the approval of any other heirs."

"It's mine!"

"No, no, my dear. If it were, you wouldn't need to hire me to contest the will."

"What do I pay you all that money for?" Her voice rose angrily. "You've fixed things for me before."

"Well," he said. "A little real estate is one thing. But this—"

"I pay you to take care of things. Take care of it!" Her words were words of dismissal, although it was she who rose, prepared to leave.

"Mrs. Soto," Florencio Apodaca said. His smile had faded, and his voice was curt and authoritative. "Do you truly want to overturn the will?" Magdalena inhaled and turned, her chest swollen as if she were on the verge of exploding. "Listen to me. If you pay good money for legal advice, you'd better take it. Into which account did you deposit that money?"

"What do you mean?"

"Into which bank account?"

"Why. Mine."

He leaped to his feet and rushed around the desk, a terrier after a Great Dane. His dark eyes flared, staring with hypnotic authority. "Do you know what the judge of the probate court would do if he knew that?" Her eyes widened, and she leaned back from him. "Do you truly want to win your case?" he repeated. She nodded mutely. "Then you'll have to play by the rules, at least some of them."

"But the money's already in the bank. What'll I do?"

"Keep quiet about it," he spat. "For all anyone knows, it's your money. Period. As for the agreement, put it away somewhere. Anywhere. Only don't tell me where. And don't tell anybody else. As far as I'm concerned, the agreement doesn't exist. If it really worries you, return it to the rancher with his deposit. Tell him you'll be back when this has gone through the courts."

"I can't do that," she protested. "We're talking about money."

Florencio bounced impatiently on the toes of his highly polished, pointed little shoes. "My dear," he said, his voice cold and venomous, "you're wasting your money when you pay me but don't listen. As administrator, you have a position of trust. The court frowns on anyone misusing that trust. If your brother knew—" Apodaca shrugged.

"Don't talk to me like that," she said. "I don't like to be talked to like that." Her eyes were red, and she was on the verge of tears. Who did this little pip-squeak think he was?

The smile came easily, too easily, as the little lawyer backed away. "My dear," he said, his voice softer now, warmer, and much more insincere. "There are certain ways that things have to be done. You have to play by the rules, by the law. We're not dealing in truth here, or even necessarily in justice. We're dealing in law. And a good lawyer has to know how to use or get around the law. I don't mean to upset you. I mean to win your case for you. But if you feel that I'm not the right lawyer, that I can't represent you to the full power of the law, then you should get another. You should get the best that you can afford."

"No," she said, shaking her head in a tight, tiny motion.

"Then leave it to me. In the meantime, if you find anything, an old letter from your father, something in his safe deposit box or in his desk, anything at all to substantiate your claim, let me know."

She nodded grimly, then turned and stomped out of the office. Without realizing it, she found herself on Gold Avenue in front of Southwest Citizens Bank. She had forgotten where Juan had parked the car, remembering it finally when she pushed open the heavy glass door of the bank. Juan can take care of himself, she thought, dismissing the automobile and driver.

Young Antonio Rafa smiled as she crossed the lobby. She ignored him. When she asked the young woman at the counter for access to Dionisio Armijo's safe deposit box, the teller apologized. She was sorry, señora, but it had been sealed by the court.

Magdalena's angry eyes measured her as for a hanging, then she hurried to Ramón Springer's office. She barged through the open door, interrupting a meeting. "I have to talk to you," she said to Springer. "Right now!"

The bank president glanced from one to the other of the employees who looked up startled at this interruption. Springer's face was alert with a premonition of trouble. "I'll just be a few minutes," he said. The man and woman left, closing the door behind them.

"Your—your teller refused to let me into my safe deposit box," Magdalena spat.

"There must be some mistake," he said.

"No mistake. The hussy said no, absolutely not."

Springer rose, took his cane from the hat rack, and headed toward the door. "Let's go see about that."

"Wait!" Springer stopped, hand on the doorknob. "I wanted to get into my father's safe deposit box," she said.

He slowly thumped back to his desk. "I'm sorry, Mrs. Soto. The court sealed it until the estate goes through probate. You'll have to get a court order to get into it."

"But there are important papers in there."

"I suggest you talk to your lawyer."

She looked at him coldly and unhappily. Surely, she thought, there are ways to get around this. All it required was a little coopera-tion. A little sympathy. But there was no sympathy in Springer's eyes. It had been he, or someone else in his family—his father?—who had told the manager to fire her when she had worked at the bank. Back then she had done as much for her customers as she now asked of the bank. There was nothing to it.

"If that's how you treat your—" she began.

"Mrs. Soto." His hands turned outward toward her in supplica-tion. "There are rules. What if someone asked to be let into your safe deposit box?" She caught her breath and looked away in alarm. "It's the law," he said.

"And my father's bank accounts?"

"The same. Protected by the courts. Although we can transfer them to the estate so it can have money for debts and expenses."

She tapped her foot impatiently. She did not take being thwarted lightly. It was personal. It had nothing to do with law. One could get around laws. It had to do with the bank. With Ramón Springer, who for some personal reason did not want to help her.

She started to smile coquettishly, but realized immediately that it would do the opposite of what she wanted. Look at that cripple! she thought spitefully. Wobbling around on one and a half legs. There is probably more than that missing from his manhood.

"I'm going to move my business to another bank!" she exploded.

Once again his hands turned outward toward her in supplication. "The laws are the same in all banks. They won't be able to do any more than we can."

"It's—it's your help!" she sputtered in frustration. "There's no respect. They don't treat customers properly. They—"

"You mean Miss Ramos?"

But she did not even hear what he said. Her frustration and anger had become sidetracked, bumping over well-worn ruts in the devious road she travelled, settling almost by chance into another rut.

"That young man!" she said. "He—he snoops into my accounts. He's spying on me. He—"

Springer sat, his face troubled, while she rattled on. When she finally stopped, breathing heavily and staring with wild eyes, he asked in a voice rasping with doubt. "What young man? I thought Miss Ramos—"

"Rafa!" she screamed. "Antonio Rafa!"

"I don't understand."

"He's— He's—" Flecks of saliva spattered from her lips, falling like tiny raindrops onto the edge of his desk. Springer's face turned blood red as he stared at her. "He's courting my niece," she spat. "He—he looked at my accounts and decided to chase after a rich, impressionable young girl. He's a gold digger. He's taking advantage of that child. He's—"

"Mrs. Soto!" He rose as if ready to leap at her and forcibly choke off the words. When she sat quiet at last, her chest heaving, he opened the door. "Send in Antonio Rafa."

Immediately Magdalena was on her feet. "I don't want to see him," she said in panic. "There's no reason—"

"Señora, those are very serious accusations."

"No," she said. "I was upset. I can't see him."

Then she began to cry, twisting her face into a dark, ugly, animal visage. Ramón Springer sighed and shook his head. The door opened. "You wanted to see me, Mr. Springer?"

"Not right now, Tony. Later."

When the door clicked shut, Magdalena looked up through red, wet eyes, anger and hate in full possession of her. Springer limped forward, clean handkerchief extended, and sat on the edge of the desk while she wiped her eyes.

"Mrs. Soto," he said. "Señora. If you are so unhappy with our service and don't feel that your confidences are being kept, you're free to move your accounts to wherever you want. I can't—I wouldn't want to stop you. I would feel very bad if you left us. Your father and mine were friends and business partners for many years. But then—" He lifted an arm and let it fall to his side, his hand slapping against his wooden leg. "Things change. Some people call it progress."

Magdalena wiped her eyes once more, then blew her nose, tucking the handkerchief in her purse. "I'm leaving," she said. "I have to think about it." Her eyes swelled, once more on the verge of tears, and her mouth twisted, barely under control. "I'm not being treated right.

Especially since my father was one of the bank's founders. There is no gratitude," she said, rising to her feet. "No loyalty."

Then she was gone, the slam of the door echoing through the quiet of marble and brass.

19

Morning Tribune

Analysis Shows Water Supply Here Is Pure

Tax Reduction Bill Agreed on in House Conference

"Oh, Papá," Leonor said. "I'm so glad you could see me."

Nicolás watched with pleasure as she looked around the dining room of the Alvarado Hotel with wide and eager eyes. She had never been here before, though she passed close by each day on the way to and from school. It was the finest railroad hotel on earth, with one of the Fred Harvey restaurants that were legendary along the route of the Santa Fe Railway. The building's towers, balconies, arches, and arcades were in the style of Old Spain. A gift shop and museum, the famous Indian Building which was a showplace of Native American craftsmanship, were attached. Through the station passed the powerful and famous of America: presidents, movie stars, Tom Mix's horse Tony.

Nicolás's eyes glistened, and he smiled shyly in awe. He could not believe that this grown-up, beautiful young lady was in some mysterious and miraculous way his child. The stiff and silent Harvey Girl waitresses watched them questioningly. He wanted to shout: "She's my daughter! You understand? Isn't she beautiful?"

"Well, hija," he said. "You told me not to come to the house. And since this is close to school and on my way to work—"

"It's so—so swank, Papá. Linen tablecloths and everything."

"Tell me. What's so important that it can't wait until my visit on Sunday?"

She reached across the table and put her small hand on the sleeve of his coat. "Papá? How old was Mamá when you married her?"

Nicolás's face grew long. He blinked his watery eyes and smiled sadly. "Just a little older than you." He spoke softly, with regret, his prominent Adam's apple bobbing up and down. "That was so long ago," he said in surprise, as if he hadn't realized it until now.

"Was she beautiful?"

"Oh, yes. As beautiful as you, my dear."

Leonor smiled, pleased at the comparison, while Nicolás waited for his daughter, his little girl who had grown up too fast, to say what he feared that she would say.

"Papá, how did you ask her?"

"Why—I just asked her."

"Did you get down on your knees and wring your hands?"

"You've been seeing too many movies."

"What did her father say?"

"Oh," he said, shaking his head. "He said all right. As long as I could take care of her. I think he was relieved. He had other daughters."

Leonor giggled nervously. "Theresa's father was relieved too," she said. "He told her she had made a good catch."

What else *could* Theresa's father say? The man was as poor as his father before him, Nicolás's father-in-law. He must have been grateful for a marriage of any kind. Especially if his pretty daughter married up in the world.

"Well," Nicolás said. "Fathers always want their daughters to marry well. To marry a man who will love them and take care of them."

The waitress set their luncheon plates deftly in place. As they ate, Nicolás watched Leonor, unable to keep from smiling. In many ways she looked so much like Mariana. Only Mariana had been a quiet little mouse, and her daughter was lively and sassy. Maybe it was the times, he thought. Flappers, women voters, free love. It was incomprehensible.

When he glanced across the room, Nicolás saw two of the waitresses look away, whispering to each other. He looked at his daughter not as a father but as a man. He knew what it was they were saying. He knew about Theresa Trujillo, heard it from the girl's drunken father bragging in a cantina. How she had trapped that boy. How she had marched up the aisle in white, her abdomen proclaiming the lie to all in church.

"Leonor," he said. "Is—is everything all right?" She looked up from her plate puzzled. "I mean . . . you're not in trouble or anything?"

"Trouble?"

"You know." God, could he bring himself to say it? To his own daughter. To his little girl. "With . . . a boy?"

Her face flushed, and her mouth dropped open. "Oh, Papá—no! Tony would never—"

"I'm so relieved," he said in a rush.

"Oh, Papá—" She patted his hand and looked away in embarrassment. "Is that what you thought I wanted to tell you?" When he did not answer, she went on. "Oh, Papá. No. I want you to meet him. Tony is such a—such a wonderful person. He reminds me of you."

What did Leonor know of him? That he had been an absent father for most of her life? That he had been loyal to her mother? Perhaps that appealed to the romantic in her. Young girls were very romantic. That he was an ineffectual man who had never succeeded at anything? But she would not know that. She would only see the outward signs. The lack of force of which Nicolás was only too aware; gentleness, his daughter would call it. The lack of practicality, which would feed her romantic fantasies. He did not know what she meant when she said Tony reminded her of him, but it made Nicolás very uncomfortable.

"I'll have to meet this young man of yours."

"That's why I wanted to see you, Papá. I want to bring him over on Sunday, instead of you coming to visit me."

He felt a pang of uncertainty, of jealousy, but he nodded. "Oh, you're just going to love him, Papá. He's so—so—wonderful. And," she continued hesitantly, "there's something else." He watched as the waitress cleared the plates and Leonor ordered dessert. "I need your advice." What advice? If not a boy, what was there big enough, important enough, for her to consult her father?

"What is it, Hija?"

She looked sheepish. "You won't be angry, Papá?" How would he know until she told him? "It's about Auntie Magdalena." She leaned toward him and lowered her voice. "Is it true that she's been married three times?"

"Why . . . yes."

"She's never talked about it."

"It's not something one brags about."

"Papá, I'm going to graduate next month. I can go out on my own."

"Yes," Nicolás said.

"If— Well, just suppose that I wanted to leave Auntie's house. Do you think I could stay with you for awhile?"

"Why of course. But why would you want to leave your grandfather's nice comfortable home?"

"I— It's hard to explain, Papá. But— You see. It's Auntie. You wouldn't know her. She's acting very strange."

Had it taken all this time for Leonor to see her aunt clearly? A heaviness came over Nicolás. He felt remorse for leaving the upbringing of his daughter to someone else. He had been so bogged down in guilt and his own convenience that he had never really considered what kind of an influence Magdalena would be on a young child. Now, he realized, that thought should have filled him with terror. My God! What had he subjected his dear, sweet daughter to? What if she had not been the stalwart young lady that she was and had given in to her aunt's influence? Or had she?

"It's hard to explain, Papá. Except that she does not care at all for Tony. She actually forbade me to see him. Well—" she said indignantly, implying how ridiculous that was. "She hasn't changed her mind, although she knows I see him. Now she tells me that he's a spy. That he's at the bank to snoop into her finances. That he's just a gold digger."

If Leonor had not been so adamant, so indignant, Nicolás would have been amused. It did not surprise him. He knew Magdalena well. "And he wants to marry an heiress," Nicolás said, more matter-of-fact than teasing.

"Why no, Papá. What do you mean?"

Her reply surprised Nicolás. Didn't she know? Had Magdalena kept that a secret too? "Your grandfather's house," he said, "will be yours some day."

"I don't understand, Papá,"

"Didn't Magdalena tell you?"

"Tell me what?"

"My dear," he said, filled with indignation. "When your grandfather died, he left a will—"

"Leaving everything to Auntie. But why didn't he leave you anything, Papá? It isn't fair!"

"Is that what she told you?" Leonor nodded. That lying thief! he thought. "Well, it's not true!" His voice rose angrily in the sudden brief interlude of quiet in the dining room. Nicolás looked around in embarrassment, then leaned toward Leonor and lowered his voice.

"Your grandfather left the house to your aunt in exchange for taking care of him these last years. It was a business transaction, pure and simple. Like buying a sack of beans at the grocery store.

"In his will he left everything else in his estate, and it was considerable, to be divided equally between your aunt and me. There was another provision, an important one. Anything from your grandfather's estate that remained when your aunt and I died was to go to you. The house, the property he owned, any money left unspent. My dear, you are an heiress."

Leonor was confused. "But she said it was all hers."

"She hired a lawyer to try and break the will," Nicolás said. "She would like it all to be hers. Your grandfather did name her administrator of the estate," he said sheepishly. "She is shrewder about money than I am. But that doesn't mean it's all hers."

"Oh, Papá. I'm so confused. I thought I knew her, but suddenly I don't."

"I want to give you fair warning, Leonor. Don't trust her. Not one bit."

Leonor's troubled face reddened, and her mouth puckered tentatively. "All the more reason to move in with you, Papá. Right away."

Much as he was willing, much as he owed her, much as he would enjoy her company, a thought stopped him. "Hija," he said. "I know it's hard on you, but until this is settled in court, we have to watch Magdalena like hawks. She's capable of anything. Maybe," he said, uncertain of how she would react, "it would be better for you to stay and keep an eye on her."

"You mean be a spy?"

"No. I mean watch out for your interests. Your future is tied to her, not in the way you may have thought, but nevertheless it is. In this world there are always people willing and eager to take what belongs to you. Even your own family. Lord knows I've met enough of them in my business dealings. Maybe I've even been a fool. But I don't want that for you."

"I don't know if I could stand being with her, knowing what I know. It's like she's been living a lie all these years, and I didn't realize it."

"It would only be for a while longer. But it could make a difference for the rest of your life."

She folded her napkin and placed it on the table beside the untouched dessert. "If you really think so, Papá."

"If it gets too bad, you can always come stay with me. There's nothing that would please me more."

She was confused now, and she looked around the restaurant as if searching for an answer. "I'd better go, Papá. I have to get back to school."

Nicolás left money on the little tray and followed Leonor. It had not turned out the way he expected. She had met him with such expectations and excitement about her young man. Now she moved slowly, wearily, laden with a previously unexpected burden.

"I have my car," he said. "Let me drive you."

"No thank you, Papá. I'll walk. I need to think."

He stood in front of the restaurant and watched her trudge toward Central Avenue, toward school, his heart as heavy as hers.

20

Evening Journal

Hoover Faces Acid Test of
His Candidacy in Ohio Primaries

Bill Haywood I.W.W. King, Dead in Russia

"I had gone outside to the privy," Magdalena said, "that's when I called for Lupe." The housekeeper nodded, watching Florencio Apodaca with intense suspicion, as if he were about to conjure up some medicine man's trick.

"But your father has been dead for over two months," Apodaca said.

"Just listen!" Magdalena said impatiently.

"I was in the kitchen," Lupe said. "I never heard such screaming in my life. 'Lupe!' she yelled. 'For God's sakes, come here!' "

Magdalena shot a look that silenced the housekeeper. "I called for Lupe," Magdalena went on. "I was standing beside the ditch—"

"She was waving this piece of paper," Lupe interrupted.

"Shut up!" Magdalena snapped.

"But it has been over two months," Apodaca insisted.

"Yes. Over two months." The lawyer nodded, satisfied. "There was a mail order catalog on the wooden seat. It had all its pages when father died, but it was slowly being used.

"It was then that I found that." Magdalena pointed to the paper on the lawyer's desk. "I tore a page from the catalog, and there it was. With writing on it."

Apodaca turned to Lupe. "Did you see it between the pages of the catalog?"

"No, señor. I mean, you know, when anybody goes out to the little wooden house they go in private. There's a hook on the door so you can latch it from the inside. No. I never saw it until she waved it at me."

"It's dated a week before Father died," Magdalena said. "He told me that he was leaving everything to me. I couldn't believe it when his lawyer read the old will."

"Why would he put it in a catalog in the outhouse? Why didn't he deal with his lawyer? Or keep it in his desk in the house? Or—"

"Are you saying that I'm lying?" Magdalena said indignantly.

"No, señora. I'm just asking questions that the court will ask. Your father was an experienced businessman, a shrewd man, who made money in sheep, started a bank, owned property. All of his business went through the same law office for years. I know Señor Vigil. He's a respected member of the bar."

"I found it there," Magdalena insisted. "As God is my witness—"

"Is this his handwriting?"

Magdalena jumped to her feet. "What kind of a question is that?" she exploded. "You'd better be sure before you go around accusing people."

"Is this his handwriting?" the lawyer repeated.

Magdalena dropped back onto her chair. "Of course."

"I don't understand how it got into the outhouse."

"I saw her when she went out of the house," Lupe said. "She didn't have it. When she yelled at me from the ditch, she had it."

Magdalena's patience was strained. She found it difficult to keep from cursing at the obstinate fool. "The only way it could have gotten there. My father. He was an old man. He hadn't been well for some time. He forgot things. He drank too much. Maybe that's where he was going the night he fell into the ditch and drowned."

"I was there," Lupe said. "She didn't have it when she went out of the house, but she had it when she yelled from the ditch."

"Yes, yes," the lawyer said.

"That's why I brought Lupe," Magdalena said. "Because she was there and saw the whole thing."

"Yes, yes. I understand." Apodaca picked up the handwritten will. He reread it, studying it intensely as if, with luck, he might be able to penetrate the scrawled words to the truth. There was only one signature. No witnesses.

He replaced the paper on his desk. "We have to take good care of this. When the time comes we can file a petition with the court. If you want, I can keep it in my office safe."

Her hand reached across the desk and snatched it up in a quick, emphatic motion. "I'll keep it."

"As you wish, señora." Then Apodaca turned to Lupe. "When this gets to court, you will have to testify."

Lupe's face clouded with fear. She looked from the lawyer to her mistress as if searching for escape. "What do you mean testify?" she asked in a trembling voice.

"Appear in court under oath that you will tell the truth."

"You mean judges and police and all that?"

"The probate judge. No police."

"You mean lawyers and things like that?" Apodaca nodded. "I don't know," she said. "I—I don't think I could do that."

"What do you mean?" Magdalena said.

The housekeeper turned helplessly, her look of fear deepening. "I don't like all that court and lawyer stuff. I'm just a poor old woman—"

"You would just have to say what you've said here," Magdalena said. She was livid, and she felt like striking the old fool.

"But I already said it. I don't see why I have to say it again. What difference would it make?"

"Look," Apodaca said. "We don't have to settle this now. What you'd better do now is talk to Alfonso Vigil. He will want to see this new will. He may even want to keep it. He has the old one."

Magdalena stiffened. "You're supposed to be my lawyer."

"Vigil represents the estate. The new will affects the estate. He has to know. I will still represent you. Your brother will no doubt contest this new document. Nevertheless, you have to talk to Vigil."

Magdalena folded the piece of paper and placed it in her purse. "Come along, Lupe. There's nothing more we can do here."

21

Morning Tribune

Anniversary of Lindbergh's Famous Flight

"Love" with John Gilbert and
Greta Garbo at the Sunshine

"Do you think he liked me?" Antonio asked. Leonor, who sat beside him in the parked coupe, entwined her arm in his and squeezed. "I mean it," Antonio said. "I already know how your aunt feels. I don't want all of your family against me."

"He was crazy about you, Tony. Couldn't you tell?"

"No."

"Well I can. He liked you very much."

"He was awfully quiet."

"That's just the way he is."

"He kept asking about my job."

"He wanted to be sure you could support me. A father who loves his daughter has a right to know that."

"He isn't at all like your aunt. I can't believe that they're brother and sister. Do you know that she tried to have me fired?"

Leonor was outraged. It was almost worth it for her aunt to attack him just so Leonor could come to his defense.

"She came in the bank the other day and raised hell when Sophie Ramos wouldn't let her into your grandfather's safe deposit box. Only instead of Sophie it was me she wanted fired. Can you beat that?"

Tony did not always understand why older people did the things they did. He *could* understand disagreement. Like with his father. When he told his father that he didn't want to be a farmer, his father had taken it as a personal rejection. He didn't mean it to be personal.

Things changed, but his father didn't want to acknowledge that. As for Leonor's aunt, he shook his head in confusion. There was no reason why she should take such a dislike to him. He, the friendly Tony. The boy that girls' mothers always liked—more than the girls themselves sometimes. He knew the latest songs, the latest dances, the latest movies. He was up on everything new. A truly up-to-date young man with a bright future.

He realized, as Leonor sat there, that her aunt had said something. Something bad. "What is it?" Tony asked. "Tell me the worst."

"Oh, I'm so confused."

"Out with it."

Her eyes moistened. Her sweet young face was tight and strained. "She warned me about Theresa," she said.

"But she's your cousin."

"She— It's—the fast crowd she runs around with."

"Wha-a-at?"

"Everybody in town knows that Theresa and José had to get married. Auntie knows that you're a cousin of José's, so—"

Well, didn't that just take the cake! "So we're the fast crowd," he said indignantly.

"Oh no, Tony. I know that's not so."

"Doesn't she see me in church every Sunday? What does the woman want?"

"It's—it's just that old people don't understand. About love. About freedom. About anything."

"So that's what she has against me. That I see José and Theresa. Well, José and I are not only cousins, we went to normal school together. We were both going to be teachers except that we changed our minds. Las Vegas Normal is the best teachers' college in the state. Better than the university. Your aunt's got her nerve!"

"Tony, don't be angry."

"And Theresa's your cousin too. Your very own cousin."

"I told you Auntie was crazy."

"And that's what she has against me? That?"

Leonor sat as if she dared not breathe. There was a stubborn set to her. Like when she didn't want to go to the movie that he suggested. Or didn't want to sit out a dance at Old Town Social Hall. He could feel the silent waves of secrecy slither down to dark, hidden places.

Places where he would not be allowed. He unfurled his arm from around her and pulled stiffly against the car door.

"Don't be angry, Tony. I can't stand it when you're angry."

"You'd better tell me," he said. "Whatever it is."

For a moment he thought that she was going to cry. He had never seen her like this. It distressed him terribly. He would do anything in the world for her. Even tell her *not* to tell him if she didn't want to.

"At the bank," she faltered. "Do you know everything that goes on at the bank?"

"What do you mean?"

"You know. How much money people have and all that."

It felt as if the car clutch had slipped, and it had lurched unexpectedly, although he knew that the car stood perfectly still.

"That's private business. We're not allowed to discuss it. With anyone."

"I mean, do you know what my aunt has in the bank? That sort of thing?"

"I'm not a snoop," he said. "I see numbers all day, but I don't remember them. I don't connect them with people. They're just numbers. It's just a job."

"But if you wanted to could you?"

"Is that what your aunt said, that I'm snooping into her business?"

"Could you, Tony?" She was close to tears.

"Yes. If I wanted to."

"Would you?"

"Of course not. It's against the rules."

"I mean, what if it was important?"

"What is it, Leonor? I don't understand."

Then she told him, her little hands trembling. Told him about her grandfather's death. About how her aunt had claimed that Grandfather had left everything to her: the house, the money in the bank, the shares of bank stock, property. How Leonor had heard and not thought much about it at first. Until she realized that her father would be left out if Aunt Magdalena were to receive everything.

Then she told him about having lunch with her father. That Grandfather's will had left everything but the house and car to be divided equally between him and her aunt. And that when Father and Auntie died, anything left of what Grandfather had owned would go to her. She, Leonor, would be an heiress.

"And she never told me," Leonor said. "She never said one word except that everything was hers. She even did some kind of business, some big deal she was so proud of, with one of the properties that belonged to Grandfather."

While working in a bank required forgetting what one sees, there were some things Tony remembered. He remembered Magdalena Soto because she was his sweetheart's aunt. He remembered how she tried to bulldoze Sophie Ramos. And had wanted him fired. *Him!*

"I don't trust her, Tony. After all these years. She raised me as if she were my own mother. Yet, now that I think about it, I don't really know her."

"She thinks I'm seeing you because of your money," Tony said. That was what filtered through Leonor's story. The old, money-grabbing witch thought he was snooping at the bank and chasing her niece because of all that money.

"Oh, Tony. It's not true. I know it."

"Thank God. I don't care whether your family has money or not. I'm going to make enough for both of us. More than enough for both of us."

She turned and kissed him lightly. "I'd better go in."

"That's it?" he said. "There isn't any more?"

She nodded, finally looking like the Leonor he knew: relaxed, warm, sweet, and rosy cheeked. They walked hand in hand to the house. He pulled her close as he hummed the tune of familiar words:

Just Mollie and me and—

She stopped at the front door and pressed a finger to his lips to silence him.

22

Evening Journal

Two Men Held Result of Raid by Dry Agents

Coolidge Asks Abolishment of War
As Tribute to Heroic Dead

"I been looking for you, Nicky."

Nicolás looked up from the ledger and put down his pen. He nodded curtly and glanced around the office to be sure no one else had entered. Then he peered through the window. A maid pushed a cart with linens, towels, soap, and toilet paper to a cabin in back.

Nicolás was repulsed by the familiarity. The bloodshot eyes and unshaven face did not inspire confidence.

"Where you been?" he asked Trujillo.

Nicolás had tried to find him in the haunts where Trujillo schemed the larcenous petty business on which he survived. He hadn't been in the pool hall for a week. He hadn't been in the low-down Barelas speakeasy for two days. This morning the fry cook at the café for railroad laborers had poured two cups of black coffee for Trujillo, who had gulped them with an aspirin and then left. Nicolás had left messages at each of the places.

"Listen, I have to tell them today," Trujillo whined. "How about it? You got the money?"

"Who are they?" Nicolás asked.

"I can't tell you. It would be my ass. Worse than that. This isn't some goddamn game."

"You want my money sight unseen?" Nicolás shook his head slowly.

Trujillo rubbed the side of his nose. His eyes widened in startled desperation, and his voice trembled. "Look, Nicky. I'll give you my IOU. My signature for Christ's sakes." Again Nicolás shook his head. Trujillo lurched to the counter, seeing his latest deal tottering on the brink of collapse. "What do you want, hombre? Honest to God. What do you want?"

"How do I know you just won't take my money and disappear?"

"You think that? You really think that? I'm your brother-in-law. I'm letting you in on this chance to make a killing. What do you want? Just tell me. Whatever it is, I'll do it."

"I want to know who I'm doing business with. That's one thing I've learned over the years."

Trujillo leaned against the counter, exhaling his foul breath. "I already told them," he confessed. "They expect to have the money today."

"I want to know who I'm doing business with."

"Me, for Christ's sakes! Me!"

Nicolás shook his head a third time. "I want to talk to one of the people you're working with."

A sob escaped Trujillo's twisted mouth. He swallowed it quickly. "Can I use your telephone?" When Nicolás didn't respond, he said, "I'll give you a goddamned dime."

Nicolás put the phone on the counter. Then he went into the back room so he wouldn't have to listen. He heard snatches of it anyway.

"Yeah. Look. He wants to meet somebody else who's in on the deal. Yeah. I told him. Look, his sister runs that place in Old Town. That's right. He says he just wants to know who he's doing business with. Yeah. OK. What time?"

Trujillo put his hand over the mouthpiece. "How about ten o'clock?"

"Where?"

Trujillo told him and Nicolás agreed. "OK. He says OK. Ten o'clock. Yeah. We'll be there."

Nicolás went back in when the receiver clicked. Trujillo tried to smile. "You'll see," he said. "It's a cinch. These people know what they're doing. I was lucky that I happened to know somebody in Juárez and was able to set it up. We'll makes lots of money. You'll see."

After he left, Nicolás realized that Trujillo had not asked if his sister was going to buy. No matter, he thought. When he had dropped in at the café yesterday, the first thing Magdalena had grumbled was, "If it's about the estate, I don't want to hear about it."

She had hovered over her books like a miser. Squeezing every little centavo as if it were her life's blood. Thank God her nosy cashier had been out. He was tired of talking business with old Trumpet Ears listening to every word.

She didn't want to talk about it? he had thought. For Christ's sakes, she was the one contesting the will.

"You know Papá promised everything to me," she said. "But just to be generous, I'll buy you out. I don't have to. Sign a release, and I'll pay you. It will cut out all those court costs. Lawyers are the biggest bloodsuckers of all."

He was so shocked that he almost forgot why he had come. He had expected some kind of shit from her, but not this. She rolled off a number that was generous for her, though it was just a small part of what their father had left. It made him suspicious. She never gave anything away.

"Well," she said when he didn't respond. "Don't you think it's fair?"

"I came to talk about a different kind of business."

She became wary. People weren't supposed to ignore her offers. He guessed that she had settled it in her mind already. She was the generous sister, trying to help her poor, downtrodden brother. When beggars refuse a handout, something is wrong. It's against human nature. It violates one of the prime rules of the universe: Greed.

"Business? What kind of business?"

"Liquor," he said, lowering his voice.

She stiffened, looking around as if the café walls were listening. "I run a respectable place. I don't know what you're talking about."

Oh, Jesus, he thought. Are we going to have to go through this? But she was alert for all her protestations. "Maybe you know someone," he said. "You're in business here. You know what's going on in Old Town."

"Maybe."

He leaned across the table and told her whispering so the help in the kitchen wouldn't hear, though, God knows, they knew they were working in a speakeasy. There was this shipment of quality liquor on its way, he said. Through luck and connections, he owned a piece of it. But he needed money. So he was trying to turn it over quickly. It was good stuff. The best. From Canada. The first person he thought of was his sister. She knew good liquor. She only served the best. And she knew a bargain. A real bargain.

When he quoted a price, her eyes brightened. "How big is the shipment?" When he told her, the edges of her mouth twisted into that Let's-see-how-I-can-bamboozle-him look. "How do I know it's any good?" He would bring her a bottle as soon as it arrived.

His heart pounded while she thought it over. He could almost hear her brain clicking like the Santa Fe speeding along the tracks. Her eyes registered dollar signs.

Finally, she cracked a smile. "For the right price I might take it all."

When she quoted a number, Nicolás remembered the pained expression he had practiced in the mirror. Tiny red blood vessels clouded the whites of his eyes.

"Look," he said desperately. "I won't make any money at that price. And I'm taking a risk." Had he overplayed it? Had he sounded too desperate even for him? Her eyes narrowed calculatingly. She thought she had him trapped with no way out. "I couldn't do it for that," he said. Then he countered high enough that she could split the difference, have the last word, yet leave him his profit.

"All right," she agreed.

"Only it has to be cash," saving this for last. "On delivery."

She hesitated. "I have to have a sample first," she finally said.

He hurried away before he did something foolish like laugh and shout hooray. She was willing to buy the whole shipment! For cash on delivery! He would make enough for the down payment on the motor court. His sister would make enough so that she could afford to pay him a settlement two or three times what she had offered.

The telephone interrupted his reveries. "Wigwam Motor Court," he answered. "Modern conveniences in a historic Old West setting."

23

Morning Tribune

Predict Woman Will Be Put on a
Major Party Ticket in 1932

Spelling Bee Winners Received by President

Never had there been such an opportunity for gain. It loomed at a time when Magdalena was pulled by the negatives in her life: the mysterious telephone calls that woke her in terror, the cantankerous behavior of her niece who became more like her impossible grandfather every day, her renewed fears of her ex-husbands whom she had not seen in years.

But the prospect of gain swept aside all such thoughts. Her father's estate would be hers, and she had already sold some of the property for a handsome sum. Her simpleton brother had come begging for her to take some liquor off his hands that she would turn into a tidy sum. It was a good thing that her lawyer had told her to go slowly on the new will. If Nicolás had known, he would never have come to see her.

It was miraculous how the prospect of gain soothed irritations, brushed aside problems, gave her an inner sense of security. When younger, she had thought that a husband would be necessary to calm her fears and help her face the future. The foolishness of youth! Husbands were no substitute for money. With enough money, all things were possible. Peace of mind was automatic. People who had snubbed her in the past could in turn be snubbed. Whatever she wanted she could buy.

Yet, for all her bravado, for all her manic pretensions that occasionally convinced her that life was wonderful, for all the false cer-

tainty with which she faced each day, there was one small corner of
her soul that trembled. It ached with uncertainty, crying out for
something more. What that something was she didn't know, even
when she allowed herself to ponder it.

For a while she thought that friendship was it. She basked in her
cashier's fawning attention, confided to her all her accumulated
knowledge of the ways of men. It was wonderful to be admired, to be
listened to, to have your words remembered.

But why was it that when people got too close they began to take
liberties? Took things for granted. Somehow the barrier of distant
decency collapsed, and one was brought down to a common level.
People became too sure of themselves, and nothing irritated Magdalena more than people who were too sure of themselves—unless it was
people who were too unsure. Like her brother. People who trembled
in the presence of authority. Who were so disgustingly inferior that
their boot-stained tongues hung out, slavering. All she could think of
was to punish them.

But now, it was the indiscreet, the too familiar attitude of her
cashier that changed Magdalena's feelings to animosity. At least
that's what Magdalena told herself. She did not admit to jealousy. Her
definition of jealousy was that people were taking advantage of her.
They were not keeping their word. They were disloyal.

The cashier's disloyalty crossed the boundary of forgiveness when
the woman pleaded illness one day. Not only did Magdalena have to
be cashier, but that night the after-hours operation was closed, and
they had planned to have dinner and see a movie. It had been a long
time since Magdalena had had any fun.

Leonor refused to go. Magdalena even considered asking Lupe,
but Lupe was in a bad mood because her husband was drinking again.

She went alone. The half-drunk Juan careened through the
streets of New Town and deposited her at one of the better restaurants. He promised to return in an hour, while she watched in anger,
imagining the low dive he would stumble into and wondering whether
or not her car would return intact.

The headwaiter approached with reserve. He glanced around for
her companion. Women dining alone were still a rarity. But it was
more than his unwelcome manner that turned her away. The back of
a familiar head shook with laughter. A familiar voice squealed at some
inanity as a woman's hand reached across the table onto the arm of

the mustachioed man. It was a knife thrust. She left without a word, hailing a taxi to scout the streets for a Packard sedan. She sent the driver in when she saw the black monument parked among wrecks in front of a pool hall on south First Street. She rode home in bitter anger and ate alone. Lupe had gone. Leonor had disappeared.

I will change my will! she raged. I was going to leave something to that cashier, but not now. What she'll get is fired. I'll leave it all to— Her mind went blank. To whom? Not to her niece, who had snuck off the minute she was out of the house. Not to her brother; he had already gotten more than he deserved. She would leave it to— No one! And she sat in frustration with a blank sheet of paper and a pen, as hot tears ran down her cheeks.

That night in bed, she waited almost hopefully for the telephone to ring. Even a ghost's haunted voice would have been welcome. But the ghost did not call, and she lay awake until she heard Leonor quietly sneaking in. The anguish froze in her breast. She realized that all of her life she had known deep down that she was alone. That whatever there was to life she would have to take. It would not be given to her. By anyone.

The realization did not calm or soothe her. But it did not enrage her either. It did not bring sleep, but it made wakefulness more tolerable. The rustle of covers from the next room did not disturb her. The slow shift of light that she sensed through closed eyes passed over her with calm inevitability.

Is this all the peace I'll ever know? she thought. Is this the only choice I'll ever have? She could not quite bring herself to say: I'll take it.

The next morning the blank sheet of paper was still on her desk with the pen beside it. She unlocked the center drawer and took out the new will. How flimsy the lock, she thought. She did not trust her lawyer, but his safe was stronger.

After Leonor left for school, Magdalena leaned out the back door. Juan was studying the yard as if deciding what task to avoid next.

"Get the car ready!" she hollered. "I'm going into town to Florencio Apodaca's."

24

Evening Journal

Athletics and Yanks Split Doubleheader
Babe Ruth Hits 14th H.R.

Dance Tonight. Music by Gere's Orchestra. Selva's.

"I saw it," Tony insisted. "The regular was out sick, and I was working the safe deposit boxes. Mr. Apodaca's secretary came in with a stack of papers. Their office safe was full, and she was transferring some things to their box. She gave me the key and the papers to take to the vault while she gossiped with one of the tellers. That woman is very careless."

"Oh, Tony, you're not supposed to look. Those things are private."

"I couldn't help it. When I set the stack down to unlock the box, there it was, right on top. Handwritten and signed by your grandfather. Dated the week before he died."

"Then it's true," Leonor said. "He left everything to her. Oh, how awful!"

"Are you going to tell your father?"

Leonor did not know. She was irritated at Tony for bringing her the bad news. Irritated at him for reading something that was none of his business. And she was also angry at her grandfather and at her aunt. Poor Father.

"There's one thing," Tony said. "I know I've been at the bank less than a year, but I've had to verify signatures and look at a lot of checks. I've gotten to know handwriting." He stopped, steeling himself. "On the one hand it looked like his writing, but on the other hand it didn't. It was just an impression. A feeling."

Grandfather had been sick for months before his death. His hands would sometimes tremble but at other times would be as steady as ever.

"Wouldn't your grandfather have left something to you?" Tony asked. "A family heirloom? Something? I mean you were very close. Closer to him than anyone. Somehow it doesn't seem right."

She tried to sort through her confusion. It was not nice worrying about what Grandfather left and who he left it to. After all, it was up to Grandfather. But yet— Why should Auntie have it all?

"If someone wanted to, how would they get a hold of it?" she asked. Tony dropped her hand and reared against the car door in shock. "Don't be holier-than-thou," she snapped. "I'm just asking a question, a suppose question."

"I wouldn't—" he began.

"Oh, stop it, Tony! Nobody's asking you to do anything."

"They put people in prison," he said.

"I'm just asking a for-instance." How could he be such a poop? she thought in exasperation. After all, he was the one who told her. "I want to know."

"There isn't any way," he said. "It takes two keys to get into a safe deposit box. The bank has a master key, and the owner of the box has a key. It's impossible to break in."

"Why did you say it didn't look like Grandfather's signature?"

"It just didn't look right. In the months before he died, every once in a while a check of his would come through that didn't look quite right. I asked Mr. Springer about a couple of them. They were for small amounts. To the grocer and things like that. He said go ahead and honor them."

Leonor sat in silence. "You're not mad at me, are you?" Tony asked.

"No," she said. But she didn't mean it.

Maybe if I talk to Auntie, she thought. But her heart contracted, squeezing ice-cold blood through her veins. Maybe Lupe, she thought. Maybe Lupe knows something. But Lupe had been acting strangely the past week. Suddenly she was palsy-walsy with Auntie, which was hard to believe.

"Don't forget," Tony said as she fumbled for her key. "They're showing *Ben Hur* at the Pastime, Saturday." She nodded and kissed him absentmindedly.

Lupe had already gone, and Magdalena was still at the café. Her civics textbook beckoned, but she resisted. She sat staring at the telephone, thinking about calling her father at work before he went to one of the places where he played guitar. What would she tell him? About the will Tony had seen? About the suspicious handwriting? God, she was behaving just like Auntie. Was she going nuts from being around Magdalena so much? No wonder her father couldn't stand Auntie. At times it was like living with a madwoman.

She turned on the radio and started to read the first of the three assigned chapters in civics. It was so boring. The book lay open in the middle of the second chapter when a key in the door roused her. Auntie walked in and looked at the clock. "You should have been in bed an hour ago," she said. "It's that what's-his-name who's keeping you up late, isn't it?"

It didn't deserve an answer. Leonor closed her book and thought: Now. Why don't I ask her now?

"Auntie, why didn't Grandfather leave anything to Papá?"

The temperature in the room dropped to wintry depths, matched by the icicle eyes that stared at her. "You should be in bed," Magdalena said.

"I can't believe that Grandfather would do such a thing."

Then, as if there was a plan, a purpose, a trio of guitars began to play over the radio, and a rich baritone voice introduced first in English, then in Spanish, a new weekly musical interlude. The soft voices in the background grew louder as the tenor sang plaintively about "El viejo amor."

"It's Papá," Leonor said in surprise. Magdalena rushed to the radio and snapped it off. "Turn it back on, Auntie. I want to hear."

"Your grandfather didn't put up with such foolishness. That's why he left everything to me."

Leonor jumped from the chair and turned on the radio. "Do you hear me, Leonor?" Magdalena said. "Life is a very serious business."

The strains of "El viejo amor" filled the room, louder now, and Leonor stood guard in front of the radio.

"Your father wasted enough money on Nicolás's foolishness. It was my turn to have something. Do you understand?"

The love song ended and another began. "Papá told me Grandfather willed everything to the two of you."

"Go to bed!"

"That when Papá dies—" She hesitated, but her aunt's angry face goaded her on. "And when you die, Auntie—whatever is left goes to me."

Magdalena barely held her anger in control. Leonor had never sensed such anger, never felt such fear.

"He put you up to it, didn't he?" Magdalena said. "That fortune-hunting bank clerk. He just wants your money, can't you see? You fool!"

"Don't you dare talk about Tony like that! I'm going to marry him! Papá already gave us permission!"

"Hah!" The scream was the bellow of a wounded animal. There was a stunned look of surprise on Magdalena's face as she sank onto the sofa.

"You never told me," Magdalena said, her voice a rough whisper. "I've been a mother to you, and after all these years you—" Winter was in her heart. Her eyes were dead like the ashes of a cold fire.

Leonor felt a pang of remorse, a flurry of confusion. "Why didn't you tell me about Grandfather's will, Auntie? How was I to know that I'm to be an heiress?"

The frozen brown eyes stared through her. "He's a spy," she croaked. "A fortune hunter."

"You never told me. Papá had to tell me."

"I'm your mother. More than your mother. The most important person in your life."

Leonor dared not respond, but silence was answer enough. She could not bear to look at the stunned woman sitting there. "You never told me," she repeated. "Papá had to tell me."

"It's a lie," Magdalena said. "Your grandfather left everything to me. I have it in writing."

But Leonor did not want to hear. Another time she might have felt sorry for her aunt. Felt the pull of what had passed for affection all these years. Instead she turned off the radio in the middle of a song. "I have to go to bed. It's late."

25

Morning Tribune

Home of Executioner Who Sent Sacco and Vanzetti to Death Is Bombed

Secondhand Store Sells Booze, Police Charge

"Ri-i-i-i-nggg! Ri-i-i-i-nggg!"

Magdalena had not been asleep. In a way it was a relief to hear the telephone. At least she no longer had to lie in bed waiting. I don't have to answer, she thought. I can just let it ring. Even ghosts get tired if you don't answer.

"Ri-i-i-i-nggg! Ri-i-i-i-nggg!" When she rolled onto her side to slide off the bed, she started to tremble. She shook so violently that she gripped the edge of the mattress to keep from falling off. Then the tears came—hot, violent tears that drenched her pillow. Hot, angry tears that she tried to will away but couldn't.

Why doesn't that girl answer? she thought angrily. Why must everything be left to me?

"Ri-i-i-i-nggg! Ri-i-i-i-nggg!"

Oh, God! she thought, finally trembling off the endge of the bed and stumbling toward the hall. She reached for the telephone like a drunk in the last stages of delirium, holding the receiver from her ear for fear of striking herself.

"There you are," the ghostly voice said.

"Who are you? What do you want?"

"This is Papá. I know what you're trying to do. I'm saving a little place for you down here. A nice, warm little place."

Magdalena dropped the receiver. It dangled just above the floor, the tinny, ghostly voice so low she could barely hear it. "I know what you're trying to—"

She turned toward Leonor's room, surprised that the door was open and that the bed had not been slept in. "Leonor?" Silence, broken only by the almost inaudible hum of the telephone. "Leonor?" She stumbled to her niece's door. The bedroom was empty.

The telephone hummed with a crackle of indecipherable words. I'm all alone, Magdalena thought. Now he can get me. She rushed fearfully to the telephone, ignoring the ghostly words, "You know who this is. I see everything you do. I know—" and hung up.

She hurried to the kitchen, the dining room, the back porch, and then again to her niece's bedroom. Leonor was gone! But how could that be? Magdalena had been awake. She had heard nothing. Then she saw the dark shape on the sofa, and she staggered toward it. The blankets were over Leonor's head. Her books were piled on the carpet. She lay still as death. Magdalena sank to the floor and put an arm across the girl's waist. She could feel the breathing, shallow and very quiet.

Let me show you, she pleaded silently. Let me get the new will from the lawyer and show you that I'm not lying. And if you'll be good, if you'll only—not love, she couldn't bring herself to think the word—if you'll only honor me. Honor thy mother— Then I'll leave everything to you. Everything!

She sat with her arm on Leonor, absorbing the warmth. Finally, she rose and removed the telephone receiver from its cradle, then made her way to bed.

Morning came too soon. She woke as if from a drugged sleep. She could tell from the light and from the sounds in the house that Leonor had already gone to school and that Lupe was in the kitchen. She looked at the clock. It was much too early to go into town. She ate a breakfast that she didn't want and couldn't taste, that slid down her throat like lumps of gall, while watching the clock and willing it to move faster.

When the time approached, she screamed at Juan to ready the car. Then she rode impatiently to her lawyer's office. "What do you mean he's in court?" she bawled at the secretary. "He can't be. I have to see him."

Magdalena looked frantically around the office, suspecting that he had hidden behind the desk or slipped under the rug. Then she burst into the adjacent office, ignoring the startled client who sat with Apodaca's law partner. "I want my paper!" she demanded. "Right now!"

Luis Perea held out a hand for his client to be still. Then the big man took Magdalena by the arm and led her out. "My will!" she said. "It's stored in your safe."

Perea motioned for the secretary as he tried to calm Magdalena, then he returned to his client. "It's on a piece of white paper," Magdalena said, hovering over the hapless woman who was dialing the combination to the safe. "I want it right now!"

She stood tapping her foot while the secretary thumbed through the stacks of papers and folders, searching frantically. "There!" But that was not it. Finally, the secretary threw up her hands. When Magdalena once again burst into Perea's office, returning with the red-faced lawyer, the secretary was on the verge of tears.

"What do you mean at the bank?" Magdalena shouted. "What bank?"

"Go with her," Perea finally said in exasperation. "Go!"

Magdalena marched out of the office, the secretary trotting behind her, and shouted at Juan. He parked across from the bank while the women marched in. The secretary searched through her ring of keys, eyes wide with fright, flipping past the safe deposit box key twice before the bank clerk reached down and plucked it free.

"You just wait," Magdalena warned, once she had the will in her hand. "This paper was supposed to be locked in your office safe. You had no business bringing it here. You," she said, thrusting a forefinger at the frightened woman who trotted through the bank beside her, "are going to get fired!"

Then Magdalena boarded the waiting automobile while the secretary stopped on the walk, burst into tears, and ran down the block toward the law office.

26

Evening Journal

U.S. Treasury Offers 4½ Percent Paper

Barelas Bridge to Be Finished by October 15

Nicolás stared bug-eyed at Alfonso Vigil. The muscles in his chest were so tight he could hardly breathe. He couldn't believe what he had heard. A heaviness settled onto him, bringing back memories. He was a child again, assaulted by that vicious sister of his. Just as he raised his fist to retaliate, she screamed, and the All-Powerful appeared from the dark to punish him.

This is just more of the same, he thought. His sister had contested the will. He was resisting. Then their father appeared from the grave with a new will that he delivered into Magdalena's hands. Now the dead man, the dead All-Powerful, would strike him for daring to oppose his little sister. Only, since dead men could not strike, the courts would do it for him.

"I—I don't understand," he stammered. His eyes pleaded to Vigil for help. "How can this be? I don't believe it." The lawyer clucked his tongue sympathetically. "Father was going to lend me the money for the Wigwam just before he died. How could there have been another will? It doesn't make sense."

"I haven't seen the document yet," Vigil said. "Mrs. Soto's lawyer informed me about it. At the same time, he said that Mrs. Soto was willing to make a generous settlement in order to avoid a lawsuit."

"The witch," Nicolás groaned. He was fighting a losing battle again; he felt it, like giant waves battering at him until he drowned.

"I told Mr. Apodaca that I would pass the information on to you, but that I represented the estate, not any one individual. I was not acting in any way as your attorney. You do have your own attorney, don't you?"

Another sin of omission. Nicolás hoped that Vigil would not notice as he ignored the question. "I just talked to her the other day," he protested. "She said something about a settlement, but nothing about a new will."

The lawyer watched Nicolás the way his father used to when he tried to talk his way out of trouble. In the eyes of the Church—and fathers—sins of omission were just as grievous as sins of commission.

"How do we know it's real?" Nicolás asked. "She's capable of anything."

"It will go through the courts."

"And Father never told you about this—this new will?"

"No."

"Apodaca said that the new will leaves everything to Mrs. Soto. There is no mention of anyone else."

"I don't believe it," Nicolás said. "What am I going to do? I just talked to that viper a few days ago. We're doing business together. She never said a word."

But Nicolás could sense that even though Mr. Vigil's expression was sympathetic, he was not too interested. "Have your lawyer call me," Vigil said. "There are some things we should talk about."

A tiny needle of guilt jabbed Nicolás. "Yes. Is that all?"

Vigil nodded. "One thing at a time," he cautioned.

It was too early in the day to go to one of his speakeasy hangouts, and he didn't have to be at work for another hour. So Nicolás walked along Central Avenue, gazing distractedly into windows until the posters screaming from one of the second-run movie houses caught his eye. "*The Natural Law.* Life's Secrets Laid Bare. Men Only. Youth Plunges in and Pays the Price in Old Age. Shows the Social Conditions of Today. Sunday, Monday & Tuesday." Then just below that: "Wednesday All Day. Special Interesting Reels. Women Only."

He turned away in embarassment when two black-garbed nuns walked by. He glanced surreptitiously at other movie theater announcements as he walked on. "*Gentlemen Prefer Blondes* with Ruth Taylor, Ford Sterling, Mack Swain. Coming next week." Then coming the first of next month at the KiMo, *Why Sailors Go Wrong*, although what really caught his eye was the current offering, the funny little man with the mustache, baggy pants, and bowler in *The Gold Rush*.

I could have gotten rich in the movies, he thought. I should have stayed in California. But thoughts of his daughter brought him to the here and now, and he felt sad and defeated again.

He stood on the corner, feeling the overwhelming need for a drink, knowing that this was not the time to have one. He settled for a cup of coffee, crossing Central Avenue to the Coney Island Café. One of his distant cousins was behind the counter, his white chef's hat flopping to the side, his white apron stained with grease and chili drippings, his muscular arms bulging in the short-sleeved shirt.

"Primo," the fry cook said. "How goes it?"

"Could be worse." The fry cook took a clean mug from the stack and waved it toward Nicolás questioningly. Nicolás nodded, and the cook filled the mug and set it down with a tarnished teaspoon and a pitcher with hardened cream on the lip.

A grizzled bum sat at the other end of the counter, staring at the handprinted signs on the wall. "Trujillo says we're all set for Sunday," his cousin said in a low voice, winking at Nicolás.

Nicolás turned on the squat stool, wishing now that he hadn't come in. Jesus Christ, he thought. Who else in town knows? "Did you see the fight last week?" he asked, hoping to sidetrack further talk of Sunday. His first sip of coffee worked its uneasy way to his stomach. His shaky confidence was fast disappearing.

The tattoo on his cousin's right bicep weighed anchor as it tightened and relaxed. "Those bums," he said. "I could have beat 'em both. At the same time. In the same ring." He smiled, his chest puffing with pride, the scars above his eyes smoothing, the gap from a missing front tooth telling of what might have been. "You go?"

Nicolás shook his head. "Had to work."

"Work? I thought you were the boss."

"Sometimes the boss works harder than anyone else."

His cousin sniffed through his flattened nose. "Not here. Hell, I don't see him from one week to the next. Especially on payday."

Two women entered, carrying bundles, and sat in one of the booths. Then the policeman who walked the beat came in for his free cup. Nicolás looked away fearfully as his foolish cousin winked while serving. He forced down another swallow and went to the register, searching through his pockets for change.

"See you Sunday," his cousin said in a low voice. Nicolás did not respond, feeling the policeman's eyes burning between his shoulder blades.

The register rang as Nicolás hurried out. He had already given Trujillo the money. It was all set for Sunday night. He would be there to collect his cash. He didn't want to know who else was involved. He already knew too much.

Jesus, he thought, wondering what that punch-drunk cousin of his was saying to that policeman. I'm going to jail!

27

Morning Tribune

Stability of U.S. Business Is Greatest in Its History

Gasoline Prices 22 Cents, Most Companies Say

Leonor sat at the front window watching the road. Tony was on his way. He had a surprise. She sat primly, barely able to control her feeling of euphoria. It was like waiting for Christmas. Or her birthday. It was a ring, she had decided. It had to be a ring.

She remembered the embarrassed glances as they had walked along Central Avenue, and she had guided him to the jewelry store windows, talking about the merits of this shape or that, of this setting or that, of where someone she knew had found the perfect little stone that wasn't really very expensive.

She shivered with delight, grateful that Auntie was at the café so she could enjoy the anticipation without a thousand questions. She had not reckoned with Lupe.

"I don't know what's sadder," Lupe said, "seeing you waiting by the window or by the telephone."

Leonor smiled, the heartrending lyrics of a popular song running through her mind:

> All alone
> By the telephone
> Waiting for a ring
> A ting-a-ling.

But the words did not make her sad. *He* was coming. *He* would be here soon. And she would not be all alone anymore. Not now. Not ever.

"Make sure you set the nice plates," Leonor said.

"Company? What's so company about him? If your aunt knew—"

"Oh, Lupe. Please."

"Well, I'm not going home until he leaves. Girls should have chaperones. Especially in their own homes."

"Did you?"

Lupe glowered and walked stiffly back to the kitchen.

At the sudden backfire of an automobile, Leonor stood and peered out the parted curtains. The little coupe careened into view, bumping along the dirt road.

"What took you so long?" she said.

"I've got it!" Tony said excitedly. He reached into his pocket and pulled out—a folded sheet of paper. "Here. Read this."

Leonor was crushed. Her eyes misted in disappointment. It was hard to keep the words in focus as she read. "Your appointment," she said listlessly.

"You don't sound very happy."

"Oh, I am, Tony. I think it's wonderful." But she did not sound wonderful.

"I have to report to Tucumcari on July first. They'll issue me a revolver, so I have to qualify before then. I'm so excited. Now we can set the date and—"

"Tucumcari? I've never been to Tucumcari. That's a long way from here." Leonor looked down at her left hand and rubbed her thumb over the inside joint of her ring finger. His excitement depressed her. It was as if his appointment were more important than her, than the wedding, than her ring! She looked at his smiling face. He was not even aware of how she felt. He seemed to look at her but not see her. Her tears overflowed.

"Honey! What's wrong?"

"July first is less than two months away. How can we do everything that has to be done?"

"We could elope. Why—there's nothing to that."

She burst out crying, her shoulders and chest wrenching. Tony recoiled, shocked by her outburst.

"I don't want to elope," she cried. "I don't want people to think we had to get married—like my cousin."

"But she didn't elope. She got married in church."

"And Tucumcari is so far away. The other end of the world. Practically in Texas, and you know what Texas is like. It's a terrible place. Mesquite and prairie dogs and dirt, like some filthy Indian pueblo."

Tony was shocked and confused. He wanted to take her in his arms and calm her, but her reaction was so unexpected, so violent, that he was afraid his touch might send her into even more irrational behavior.

"What is it, Leonor? What's the matter?" His concern finally overcame his fear, and he took her in his arms. He patted her gently and kissed her tear-streaked cheeks.

"What if robbers hold up the train?" she cried. "And—and—"

He had the good sense not to say what he thought: That he would have a revolver to take care of such things. "This isn't the wild west anymore," he said. "Who's going to hold up a train?"

She clung to him, her tears soaking his shirt. "There, there," Tony said. "Everything's going to be wonderful." He tilted her head and kissed her eyes. "How is it going to look if I take you into the jewelry store looking like that?"

"What?" she said, immediately alert. It was amazing how quickly tears could dry.

"I want you to pick your rings before they close. We have half an hour."

She unfurled herself from him, eyes bright. "We don't have much time," Leonor said. "Lupe!" She rushed to the kitchen. "We have to go into town. We'll be right back."

"But dinner is almost ready," Lupe protested.

"Oh, I look such a sight," Leonor said to Tony. "Let me wash my face. I can put on my makeup in the car."

Tony was astounded at the speed of her transformation. He shook his head, not understanding.

28

Evening Journal

Liquor Blamed for Murder by Navajo Indian

Illness Costs Each Family $134 Per Year

Leonor sat stiffly beside her aunt's desk in what she always thought of as her grandfather's office. Outside Lupe was yelling at Juan. Her aunt was sitting ramrod straight, waiting for her to say something. Leonor read the paper again and thrust it onto the desk as if ridding herself of something vile.

"I don't believe it!" Leonor said. "Grandfather would never do such a thing."

"I want you to see, young lady, that your grandfather left everything to me. For good reason. I took care of him in his old age the way I took care of you from the time you were a baby. He believed in rewarding responsibility the same as I do."

"I don't believe it!"

"And those who show ingratitude get what they deserve."

What her aunt meant was that if she was obedient and did what she was told, Auntie would be generous. What her aunt meant was that she should give in to bribery, no matter what her deepest personal feelings. Leonor wished that she did not have to wait two more days for her engagement ring to be ready. She would flaunt it at her aunt. Breathe on it and polish it. Hold it up to the light for its sparkling reflection to say: Somebody loves you. Someone dear and handsome and clever. He wants to care for you the rest of your life.

"Leonor, do you hear me?" She glared at her aunt, at the pinched, dark face with heavy devil's eyebrows, at the tight, grim mouth, at the stiff back, a drill sergeant's back, barking orders at the world.

"I forbid you to marry that fortune hunter! I will leave you nothing, do you hear? Nothing!" The threat was tinged with self-satisfaction, with pleasure in exercising power.

Leonor's smile was barely perceptible. I forbid you! she thought. I will leave you nothing! Nothing but the man she loved. Nothing but a lifetime of happiness. Everything that Auntie's money had failed to buy for her.

What Leonor realized was that she no longer had to stay and keep an eye on her father's and her own interests. She had seen the new will and did not believe it. It did not look exactly like Grandfather's handwriting. She knew his writing well enough. For the past year she had copied letters for him when his hands had trembled so much that his writing was illegible. Then he would scratch his feathery, difficult-to-read scrawl across the bottom of her handiwork.

Was Aunt Magdalena capable of forgery? Just thinking about it made her dizzy. She could not imagine anyone doing such a wicked thing. There was more than enough for her father and aunt to share.

"Answer me, Leonor! This is a very important step you're taking. It could ruin your entire life." Or save it, Leonor thought. "After all I've done for you, you at least owe me an answer."

What good would it do to tell her again? Leonor had told her already—many times. Auntie had laughed as if it had been a joke. As if Leonor was only teasing—now tell Auntie the truth. She would just leave, Leonor thought. Father said he would take her in. Maybe the house was small and in the wrong part of town. But it was close to school and far, far away from here.

"You will have to face facts, Leonor. You're not living a fairy tale."

Yes, Leonor thought. I will ask Tony to help me move the next time Auntie works late.

"Leonor!"

"I'm going to marry him, Auntie! I am!"

29

Morning Tribune

Mary Pickford Here with Doug; Worn Out by Interviews

Five-Hour Day for All Seen in Future.
British Professor Says Human Is Lazy and
All Domestic Service Will Be Relegated to Machines

Magdalena's place was well known, located off the plaza and shielded from San Felipe Church by the little adobe houses that seemed to be melting back into the earth. It stood behind the old Springer house, as if trying to borrow some of its respectability.

Nicolás had arranged for the delivery on a night when the café speakeasy closed early. The last tortilla crumb had been wiped from the tables, and the last dirty dish washed and put away at ten o'clock. Now it was midnight, and Nicolás stood confronting Magdalena in the dimly lit café.

"I couldn't get it all in cash," she said. "Most of it is here, but I have to give you a note for the rest."

He should have expected it, Nicolás thought, before a flood of desperation engulfed him. "These people have to be paid. Now! The first truckload is on its way. They'll be waiting for me to tell them that it's all right to unload. You don't play games with these people. Someone will get killed."

A sense of his desperation must have broken through her apparent indifference, but it was difficult for her to act other than the way she usually did. "That's all I have," she said. "Take it or leave it!"

He could have asked her about the bank. He was certain that she had twice that amount in her account. Not to mention the estate's account, although the thought of it filled him with anger. He wanted to settle this business and get away. Before he blurted out that he knew about the new will. A forgery! he would shout, although he had not seen it. Another one of your dirty tricks!

He heard the truck in the distance, grinding towards the plaza. Although she did not show it, he knew now that Magdalena was afraid, bluffing to the very last in order to do him in. He could smell her fear. Not quite the sharp odor of roasting chili. More subtle than a wet dog lying beside a hot stove. But no soap could dissolve it. No perfume could mask it.

"Here it comes," he said. "What am I going to tell them?"

Her fear became visible. "I have some change in the register. Maybe there's enough."

But there wasn't. And feeling the anxiety almost as much as she, he took what he could, including an IOU for the small unpaid balance.

The headlights flashed into the plaza, then turned up the dirt alley to the café. Nicolás went outside. The driver, a dark man he had never seen before, had a scar across his left cheek like a miniature furrow turned over by recent plowing.

"Where's the money?" the man barked. Nicolás handed the envelope through the window. Trujillo and the cousin from the Coney Island sat next to the driver, staring over Nicolás's head as if they didn't know him. "OK," the driver said after he had counted. He slipped the envelope inside his jacket. A revolver in his waistband winked at Nicolás. "Where to?"

Nicolás jumped on the running board. "Jesus!" the driver growled. "Why do these little shithouse places have to be down an alley? We could've used the big truck otherwise. This will take all night."

It didn't. It took three truckloads, with the driver acting as lookout while the other men unloaded and Nicolás and Magdalena watched nervously. When they finished, Nicolás nodded a curt good-bye to his sister—for the last time, he had decided. He drove home, fearful for the cash and the IOU in his pocket. Never again, he told himself. No amount of money was worth the anxiety and the strain.

* * *

Two days later, just before midnight, the last visitor had slipped up to the café door, a cap stuck in his hip pocket. As usual, the small

eye-level peephole slid open to reveal a wary eye. Then the password
in Spanish, "Cipriano sent me." A bolt snapped, and the door opened
just wide enough to let in the unknown man.

The café was not recognizable in the low light. It was crowded
with shadowy figures. More tables were crammed in than usual.
Cigarette smoke hung heavy in the air that buzzed with voices and
laughter. There was no music, no dance floor. People snuck in to get
drunk, barely able to see the dark shadows at the next table, comfortable in their anonymity.

Magdalena stood behind the bar watching the bartender pour and
count out change for the waitresses. A burly man was on guard at the
door. The man with the cap drank one fast whiskey, then rose to
leave. "It's early," the guard had said. "The music doesn't start for
half an hour."

But the man adjusted his cap and waited for the door to open. As
he stepped out, a hard shoulder bumped him aside, and men rushed in.
"This is a raid!" one of them shouted. "Stay put and you won't get
hurt!" The stranger in the cap had disappeared.

The shattering sound of breaking glass started the panic. A
woman screamed, "¡Chotas!" and the place exploded. Confused,
angry, frightened patrons jumped through broken windows and
forced their way through the front door. The police were not interested in them, rushing at those working in the back.

Lights went on in a few of the houses behind the church. Frightened paisanos, rudely awakened, heard the shouts and screams fading
in the distance. Automobile tires squealed as people escaped the
cantina, speeding away with headlights off.

*   *   *

All that anyone learned was what appeared in the newspapers. An
informer had alerted the authorities. "A good citizen," the morning
newspaper had said, not indicating whether the wish for a reward or
the desire for revenge were factors.

When Eddie Carr came into the office the next afternoon, he
handed the newspaper to Nicolás. "Prohi Agents Raid Old Town
Speak," the headline read. "Proprietress and Help Arrested for Selling
Bootleg Hootch."

Nicolás scanned the article with pounding heart. He could feel

Eddie's stare. He had already seen the story in the morning paper. "My God!" He folded the newspaper and dropped it on the counter.

Eddie sighed and shook his head. "I'm sorry. It's a damned shame. I mean, what a stupid law. Everybody drinks a bit now and then, which means somebody has to sell it."

"My God!" Nicolás repeated.

The article said that when federal agents had raided the speakeasy, employees of the cantina had rushed to the storehouse and smashed bottles with axes to destroy the evidence. Agents finally had to wring the proprietress' and waitresses' dress hems, which had gotten soaked during the axing. The squeezings were submitted to a chemical laboratory for analysis.

Patrons of the speakeasy had been released after being booked. Mrs. Magdalena Soto had been released after her attorney had posted bail. Legal action against Mrs. Soto and her employees was forthcoming.

"I just can't believe it," Eddie said earnestly. But Nicolás knew Eddie too well and saw through his apparent sincerity. Eddie was a habitual gossip and never more curious than when he showed concern. "Have you talked to her yet?"

"No."

"What made her do a fool thing like that? The café was doing great. She made the best enchiladas in town."

Nicolás shrugged. Eddie was making him nervous. He wished he would go away. It hadn't occurred to him before, but he realized that federal agents would be asking Magdalena questions. Like where she got the whiskey. He broke into a sweat. If she said anything, he would be implicated. He would be arrested. He could see the headline in the newspaper: "Sister Squeals On Local Rumrunner." She was capable of it; he didn't doubt that. He was at her mercy again, the cross that he would have to bear forever.

"Did she ever let on to you what she was doing?"

"No." Eddie smiled disbelievingly. "We don't even get along. She's suing me."

But all the time Nicolás was thinking: What is she going to say? Would she tell where she got her liquor in order to save her own skin? Yes, he answered. But then, she had been serving liquor at the café for months. She had other sources, regulars from the local bootlegging community. What would her life be worth if she turned them in? No, he thought. The Canadian shipment was only a small part of the picture. Why report just that source?

"You'll have to help her," Eddie said. "After all, family is family." He picked up the newspaper and shook is head sympathetically. "I'm sorry I had to be the one to bring you the bad news. If there's anything I can do, anything at all—" Eddie slapped the folded newspaper on his thigh and left.

Nicolás watched him amble up the drive toward the rear of the court. He wasn't about to talk to Magdalena. He wished he could disappear until the mess was over.

The telephone rang. He stared, trembling, not wanting to answer. It had to be a customer, he decided, so he picked it up after the fourth ring.

"It's all your fault! You're going to have to get me out of this!" It was Magdalena.

"We can't talk," he said quickly. "What if someone is listening?"

"If it wasn't for you—" She was on the verge of hysteria. "You'll have to meet me someplace. Right away."

"I'm working."

"I want my money back! You owe me that!"

He wanted to slam down the receiver, but if he did, she would telephone the prohibition agents. He felt nauseous, and the pit of his stomach burned like when he ate too much hot, green chili.

"We can talk Sunday when I come to visit Leonor."

"It's your fault! I want my money!" And she hung up.

Nicolás replaced the receiver cautiously, wondering if her telephone was tapped. Federal agents were probably watching her house, taking notes on who came and went.

He reached into his wallet for the IOU tucked in among the bills. He dropped it into an ashtray, struck a match, and watched it flare up, curl, and disintegrate into black cinders.

30

Evening Journal

Aviatrix Earhart on Transatlantic Flight

Income Less in New Mexico Than Elsewhere

Alfonso Vigil had told him the news, but Nicolás had not really understood and could not decide whether it was good or bad.

"I've petitioned the probate court to freeze the assets of your father's estate pending an investigation. Mrs. Soto sold some land that belonged to the estate and took a cash down payment."

"Land? What land?"

"She never spoke to you about this?"

"No."

"She's supposed to get your agreement before she can sell anything."

Now it dawned on Nicolás, but it did not seem too important anymore. Nothing did. Not even buying Eddie Carr's share of the Wigwam. What was land compared to prison?

"But what about the new will?"

"It hasn't been validated. The estate is still being administered under the old will. She violated her trust as administrator. The court will do something about that. She won't be able to write checks or sell property anymore. And it raises questions about her lawsuit.

"Of course," Vigil continued, clasping his hands across his stomach like a Buddha, "her new difficulties with the law raise other questions."

Nicolás's insides froze. He did not want to talk about his sister's arrest. The lawyer cleared his throat and waited silently until it was obvious that Nicolás was not going to talk.

"I will have to say that it makes it better for you," Vigil finally said.

A question struggled into Nicolás's mind, fighting through his anxiety like a bird lost in a storm. "How did you find out about the land?"

Vigil grunted. "The buyer told the court appraiser when he drove out to look at it. The cash was never deposited into the estate's account. It should have been."

The bank? Nicolás thought. Where will I put my bootleg cash without arousing suspicion?

"It's going to take awhile to untangle all this," Vigil said, "but in the long run you should come out all right."

Of course, Nicolás thought. If it all goes right, I'll be a rich man when they let me out of prison.

*   *   *

"I'm sorry to bother you at work, Papá, but I can't stand it here anymore. I feel bad about Auntie's troubles, but I wanted to leave before. Anyway, there's nothing I can do. She's changed. I think she's losing her mind. Why else would she get into that mess at the café? I had no idea she would do such a thing."

"When are you coming?" he asked.

"I don't know, Papá. Soon. I used to know what nights Auntie would be at the café, but now that it's closed, I don't know. She stays home and drinks. It's terrible. Tony will come get my things, but I don't know exactly when."

"If I'm at work, stop here for the key."

"Oh, Papá. How can I thank you?"

Nicolás glowed. No thanks were necessary. He realized that Leonor did not think badly of him after all the years they were apart. That there were ties that time and distance could not sever, a thin unbreakable thread of love that would grow even stronger the more they were together.

"One thing more, Papá. Tony bought me an engagement ring."

"How wonderful."

"He got his appointment from the government. He has to be in Tucumcari by July first. We're going to get married. We'll tell you all about it when we see you."

Everything was moving too fast. His little girl was an engaged young woman whom he hardly knew. He was an old man whose youthful dreams had never been fulfilled. Now he doubted that they ever would.

Well, he thought, she shall have a proper wedding. That's one thing a father is good for.

He looked around the office. At the out-of-date magazines on the table. At the printed sign on the wall behind the counter: "In God we trust. All others pay cash." At the membership plaque from the Chamber of Commerce. At the ashtray beside the telephone. At the cheap framed prints of Indian pueblo life on the walls.

Better to give Leonor a good send-off, he thought, than to own half of this, much as I want it. He repeated the words, still looking around. He had no regrets.

31

Morning Tribune

Albuquerquean Fatally Hurt in Fall under Car

Fall, Doheny to Face Trial for Bribery, Says Teapot Leader

Magdalena was in a panic. She had spent much of her life building an impregnable fortress between herself and the hostile world that lay waiting to get her. Now it was as if the drawbridge had been let down by a traitor in her camp, and the savages were attacking. She should have heeded the first sharp howling of coyotes when Nicolás came back to stay. Instead she had watched the wolves slinking quietly closer, not noticing the sharp, biting growl of mountain lions that should have told her that all the wild creatures in the forest were moving in.

But I have money, she thought. That will protect me.

Then she thought: Maybe I don't have enough. That must be it. I don't have enough. If I have to pay every wolf who comes sneaking up on me, there may be one too many. Or a mountain lion may follow. It will be that one, the one I can't pay, who will undo me.

Like Nicolás, she thought. Although it strained belief to see Nicolás as a wolf or a mountain lion. But it was his fault. If he hadn't come to her with that offer of Canadian whiskey, she would not be in trouble now. She should never have listened to him. Never agreed to take the contraband off his hands. She should have known better. Had he ever succeeded at anything in his life? Everything he touched turned to shit. Why had she listened? It was his fault. He owed her!

And Papá, she thought, angry rather than fearful of thinking ill of the dead. You were the one who taught me to be shrewd. Who taught me that the rules only apply to ordinary people. Why didn't you warn me? What good are your teachings now?

She did not consider that life had taught her father a hard lesson when he had been driven from political power for bending the rules too much. She did not see that this had been the beginning of the end for him.

Then, too, he had been telephoning from beyond. He said he was saving a nice little warm place for her. Where he didn't say. She shuddered, rejecting the thought of hell. Wondering if heaven had its nice little warm places.

But he had not telephoned for awhile, she realized in surprise. Not that she missed the ghostly voice. It struck terror into her heart. She still lay awake nights fearful that the telephone would ring although it hadn't for days. The mere thought of it reawakened unknown fears— something secret, ominous, vicious, was waiting for the right moment to do her in.

Since she did not understand newfangled gadgets like the telephone and radio and automobile, it seemed perfectly reasonable that ghosts should communicate through them. At times the ghostly voice was almost like that of some live person whom she knew. It would have been more terrifying if the voice came out of the invisible air. That would be truly supernatural.

In her panic, she found more than enough blame to pass around. It did not stop with her brother and her father. There was enough for the women in her life. For her dead mother, that silent doormat who lived her last years wallowing in religious fantasies. That woman who had been out of touch with the child, Magdalena. The woman who for some inexplicable reason championed Magdalena's rival, Nicolás. For Magdalena had never realized that she had been her father's favorite when small. That he had spoiled her unbearably. She had accepted his spoiling as her just due. And she never realized that her mother's reaction had been one of trying to right the imbalance. What her father had given to Magdalena, he had withheld from Nicolás. Oh, Mother, she thought, wanting everything from both parents: Why didn't you love me?

Somehow that lack of love had passed from mother to mother's granddaughter, Leonor. For all that Magdalena had given her niece— she had actually been a mother to her—she had been repaid with disloyalty. Like her mother, her niece had turned instead to Nicolás, bestowing on that—that worm—what Magdalena properly deserved. Why was it? When people worked hard for money, they got it. Why didn't the same thing happen when they worked hard for affection? It was perverse. As if love was something that could not be earned. As if it was some essence floating in the air like ghosts, making its visitations whimsically on whom it pleased.

Even showing the ingrate girl her grandfather's will, even asking for no more than a little cooperation, did not dent her stubborn resistance. The hell with her! The hell with them! All of them! I don't need them! At which she lurched toward the kitchen cabinet where she kept her liquor.

"Lupe!" she shouted. "Where's the whiskey?" She slammed the door of the empty cupboard and looked around the kitchen angrily. She stumbled to the back door. "Lupe!"

"Sí, señora."

"Have you been drinking my whiskey?"

"No, señora."

"Then where is it?"

"What you didn't drink, you hid. You told me you didn't want them to search the house and find it."

Magdalena weaved unsteadily, trying to remember. "Where did I hide it?" she asked suspiciously.

"You told me you didn't want me to know."

The housekeeper's impassive face did not fool Magdalena. She knew what Lupe was thinking. That it was a good thing that the liquor had been hidden where she couldn't find it. That liquor had been the family's downfall, what with her father's death and now jail looming for her.

"The front of the house is a mess," she snapped. "There are papers all over. Clean it up!"

Lupe turned without a word and headed into the house.

"Where's Leonor?" Magdalena screamed.

The housekeeper answered without turning around. "At school. Graduation practice."

The telephone rang, and Magdalena's heart clenched, then unclenched. She slammed the screen door and made her way back into the house.

"It's Señor Apodaca," Lupe called.

"Yes," Magdalena said into the telephone. "What's that? What do you mean a court order? It's mine. Father left it all to me. I have the new will."

She only half listened while he lectured her about not being allowed to sell the property and about the deposit in the bank. From now on everything had to have court approval, even a check for two cents.

"It's mine!" Magdalena protested. "They can't do that!" But deep down she felt that the whole world was against her.

32

Evening Journal

Fiesta of San Felipe Opens in Old Town

Erna Fergusson Tells of State's Spanish Folks

"I can't wait anymore," Leonor whispered into the telephone. "She's asleep. She's been drinking again. Come quickly."

She replaced the receiver carefully. Her aunt lay sprawled on the sofa snoring. Leonor closed the door to her room and checked once more to be sure that she had everything. Erratic, drunken singing floated from outside. She peeked through her bedroom window at the huge Packard, partially wet, which was parked alongside the shed. The top of Juan's hat, then his head and shoulders, emerged from behind the car. The hat was cocked jauntily as he smiled at the wet Packard. He stopped singing and tilted his head back as the bottle kissed his lips. He swallowed and sighed. He had found Magdalena's hidden liquor.

Lupe, thank God, had walked to the little store in the plaza. If only Tony would hurry she would be gone before Lupe came back. Leonor went through her clothes and books a third time, tapping a foot impatiently. She cracked open the door and peeked at the sofa. She felt remorse for sneaking off, but there was nothing she could do about her aunt's problem. It had, in fact, become Leonor's problem too. She had hated the questioning eyes at school. The heads close together whispering. The arrest was the talk of the campus, even among her teachers. She was scandalized almost to tears.

She carried her things to the front porch and stacked them beside the screen door. Then she sat and waited. The drunken singing carried faintly from the back of the house. She had decided not to leave a note. She could imagine her drunken aunt driven by the drunken Juan, assaulting her father's little house demanding that Leonor come back. I can tell her later, she thought. I don't have to tell her now.

It's taking an hour, she thought fretfully, knowing that it had been only minutes since she had telephoned Tony. Then, hours later so it seemed, she heard the purr of an automobile, and the little coupe turned at the intersection and raced toward the house.

She stood and gathered what she could in her arms, pushing her way out the screen door toward the car. "The rest is on the porch," she said in a low voice. "Hurry."

* * *

It sounded like a platoon of squeaking boots approaching rapidly. Like cheap boots from the dry goods store of her childhood that either dissolved or shrunk after being out in the first rain. What was it? Magdalena thought. So many footsteps.

She forced herself up, struggling to open her eyelids. "Lupe." No answer. "Lupe." She wiped her eyes and shook her aching head. "Lupe!" she screamed. "Where are you?"

The footsteps stopped abruptly. She turned and saw the giant cucaracha, its flat brown body pressed against the wall shrinking from her. Its long antennae were wriggling like shiny brown-shelled snakes. Its voice was a high-pitched squeak.

She was dreaming. It had to be a dream. The thought calmed her a bit. But when she wiped her eyes and pinched herself, the cockroach did not disappear.

She screamed. The creature drew back against the wall, its squeak higher pitched and more rapid.

Magdalena's immediate urge was to run, but her legs were paralyzed. "Lupe," she called, her voice a raw whisper.

The creature squeaked. The long antennae wriggled frantically, reaching toward her tentatively. The squeak wavered in pitch, every few pulses interrupted by flat, fuzzy static like that between stations on the radio. Finally she understood what it was trying to say.

"Who are you?" she asked in a hoarse voice.

"Squeak. I won't hurt you. Squeak—squeak."

"What do you want?"

"It's me," the creature said. "Can't you see? It's me." She gave an involuntary shudder. "I won't hurt you," the creature repeated.

"Who are you? What do you want?"

Her eyesight, no longer clouded by sleep, had become intensely keen, like a lens polished by fear. There was something familiar about this hideous creature. The spots of food on its shiny shell. The soft oozings of bad skin between its plates. The faint aroma of unwashed underwear. The authoritative voice, even though only her mind heard it, was familiar.

"It's me," the creature said. "Can't you tell?"

But all she could see was the hard, brown shell, shiny like dark amber. The overlapping plates twisted and turned slowly as the creature moved. The long antennae finally retreated and hung suspended above its head, watching. The eyes on the ends of the antennae were black and soulful. It stood on its hind legs, the other pairs hanging like the forepaws of a begging dog trying to imitate an upright human. But there was nothing human about it except its size, that of a man of slightly greater than average height trapped within an insect's body.

"Papá?" she said. The antennae wriggled gently in reply. "But you always telephoned before."

"Well," she heard in her mind, although all her ears heard was the infernal squeak. "I didn't want to frighten you. You wouldn't have listened."

"What is it that you want, Papá?"

"Do you remember that paper you wanted me to sign? You remember? The new will?"

"Yes, Papá."

"I didn't want to sign it," she heard in her mind. "That's why I told you that I wanted to read it and think about it."

"You hid it, Papá."

The hard-shelled head nodded slowly. "It wasn't my will, you see. It was yours. Whatever Nicolás's faults, he deserved more than that. After all, he is my son. And your brother."

"I found it, Papá."

"And you signed it. Now destroy it. Before it's too late."

"Too late for what?"

"To go to the nice warm place that I've been saving for you."

Magdalena reared against the back of the sofa. This was absurd!

What was she doing talking to this squeaking apparition? There was nothing there. No giant cockroach. No sounds translated to words in her brain. It was all imagination. Fantasy. It was what happened to people in nightmares. Or when they drank too much. And she decided that that was it. It was that cheap liquor that Nicolás had sold her. It was his fault!

"What if I refuse to go to your nice little warm place?"

The squeaking rose to such unbearable intensity that she covered her ears with her hands. "Then the other place," her mind heard. "You'll go to that squeak squeak down in the fiery squeak of squeak. Eternal. Forever. Not like the gentle squeak of the little warm squeak, but raging squeak that is unbearable, unforgiving, infinite. From the warm little place one can go up or squeak. One becomes the embodiment of what one was repulsed by in life. One becomes the target of one's own fears. Squeak. La cucaracha is the creature that all men step on, the way that I stepped on men when I was alive. So here I am. Condemned. Until that time when the Lord has mercy. And you—"

She could feel the giant cord drop over her shoulders like a lasso. Feel herself changing shape, turning green, until, suspended, a giant hand would swing her round and round on the end of the cord like the grasshopper that she had so abhorred as a girl. Or a rat, she thought, scampering beady-eyed to escape scrawny cats and poisoned traps.

"Go away!" she said. "Who are you? Nothing. Just my imagination."

"Squeak. Squeak squeak."

The antennae started to wave back and forth again, like angry, thrashing arms. Words no longer formed in her head, and the squeaking rose to a pitch of such intensity that her eardrums were ready to burst.

"Go away!" she screamed.

The antennae came nearer, touching her, and she shuddered as the hard, brittle shell bumped against her breastbone. "Go away!"

"Señora," she heard. "Señora." But it was coming from a fog. From far away. "Señora."

"Lupe. Oh, my God. I had the most awful dream."

"Are you all right, señora?"

She pushed Lupe's arm from her and sat upright on the sofa. She looked toward the far wall. Nothing there. Then she slowly searched behind the furniture and in the corners.

"How long have I been asleep?"

"I don't know, señora. I went to la tiendita. I'm getting ready to start dinner."

Magdalena looked up in alarm at a new thought. She staggered across the room to her desk and searched the top frantically. "Where is it?" she said, her voice rising. "Lupe, what did you do with it?"

"Do with what?"

"The paper. The paper that was on my desk. It was here. Right here."

Lupe's eyes widened in fear. "There was nothing on the desk, señora."

"It was here, I tell you!"

"There were papers on the floor. And on the sofa. You told me to throw everything out. But there was nothing on the desk. As God is my witness."

Magdalena turned frantically, darting first this way then that, unable to decide which way to go. "Where are they?" she screamed. "What did you do with them?"

"I burned them, señora."

"It was on my desk," she said in disbelief. "Where's Leonor?"

Lupe's face sagged. She looked away guiltily. "I should have waked you," she said. "But I didn't want to bother you. You were talking in your sleep."

"Where is she?"

"When I was walking back from la tienda I saw her in a car with her boyfriend."

Magdalena rushed to Leonor's room. The bed was stripped to bare mattress, sheets and blankets gone. She jerked open the closet door. Half of Leonor's things were missing. Her schoolbooks were gone as were the photographs of her mother and father that she kept on the dresser.

"Juan!" Magdalena shouted, rushing to the back door. "Where are you, you good-for-nothing?"

Lupe trotted behind her as she burst into the yard. "Juan!" She rushed to the car where he lay slumped in the driver's seat, snoring drunkenly. "Wake up!" Magdalena shook him. "Wake up, you bum. You miserable cabrón. She stole it. She ran away with it."

But Juan just groaned and rolled over, still deep asleep. "Help me," she commanded Lupe. "Get him out."

They dragged the drunken Juan from the car, laying him alongside the shed where he continued to snore. "The keys!" she demanded of Lupe, who rummaged through her husband's pockets. "I'm going," Magdalena said. "Call the police. No— Don't call the police. I'll be back."

She climbed into the car, hesitating a moment trying to remember how to start it. Then she climbed down to the front to crank it. "Señora," Lupe said. "Be careful."

They eloped, Magdalena thought, trying to recall the telephone conversation she had overheard between Leonor and one of her girlfriends. Where was it she said they could go? Corrales! she remembered triumphantly. The Justice of the Peace in Corrales.

The engine kicked over, and she got into the seat and peered into the rearview mirror. Although she had driven the car but once before, if that fool Juan could drive, so could she. She put it in gear and slowly backed out of the dirt drive, drifting in and out of the flower bed.

They eloped, she thought. Then God knows what they'll do with the will. That's what comes of getting involved with a fortune-hunting bank clerk. I'll kill him! she thought. I'll kill both of them!

She backed onto the road, ground the gears, then lurched forward toward Río Grande Boulevard, toward the river, toward the bridge that led west to Corrales.

Part Three

33

Old Antonio stilled his rocking chair and looked at his son who asked, "How come you never told me about this before?"

Antonio sat a moment, staring. He had become confused. Suddenly the years had overlapped, the times bumping shoulders like people hurrying along a crowded sidewalk. Then the years bounced off each other, separating once again. Still he stared, overcome by the realization that Tony was now the same age that his father-in-law, Nicolás, had been then: forty-eight. Though Tony resembled his maternal grandfather physically, being tall and thin, in temperament he was a throwback to his more volatile Rafa ancestors.

"First you were too young," he finally said. "Then when you were old enough, you couldn't wait to get away from here. You went off to the army, then to college. Now you're in California teaching. We never had the time to talk."

Tony frowned. Antonio knew that some small slight, real or imagined, had piqued him. "Has Mary heard the story?" Tony asked. The old man shook his head. "The others?" Meaning Stella and Joe. Antonio shook his head again.

"When are you coming to California with me, Papá? Good God, how can you stand it here?"

"Stand it? What is there to stand? This is my home." As if that explained everything. "Your mother and I left when we were first married. Tucumcari, El Paso, Tucson, even Los Angeles.

"There was more reason to leave then. A small town without much opportunity. You worked for the railroad or the government or you raised chili and beans. My job took me away. But your mother and I missed it. We belonged here, though we didn't know it at first. Tied to our families. To our history. I can't explain it. It's just a feeling. Something in your bones that tells you this is your home." The old man's eyes misted. "You know, I really love this place. Almost as much as I love your mother and you children."

But Tony was still pondering his sisters and brother. "You never told them? Why are you telling me?"

"You're the writer of the family. Someday you may want to write a book."

Antonio had always been a reader. Not, of course, the sort of things that college professors read. He had never heard of the writers and books that Tony talked about as if they were acquaintances one ran into in the plaza every day. His reading had been more of the daily newspaper and the pulps, like Doc Savage and the detective magazines that were no longer published.

"I'll always remember," Tony said, his mood shifting, "when you threatened to cancel your magazine subscriptions because they rejected my stories. The mailman was afraid to deliver the envelopes to the house."

Antonio smiled, gazing out from the shaded porch of the cottage toward the larger house, his old house, where his daughter Mary and her family now lived.

"Maybe I could tell the committee that we won't donate the land for the park unless they do your play."

"Hah!" Tony said. "Too late for that." He glanced at his wrist-watch. "We have to drive to the meeting soon."

Antonio was relieved. Soon it would be settled. Then he could go to the convalescent home and tell Leonor that her wishes were being carried out. One morning out of three she would understand what he said. Mostly she would sit in her wheelchair, eyes closed even when awake. She would hear him enter and open her eyes to stare at him with a puzzled expression.

"Your mother had a good day yesterday," he said.

"You mean she wasn't out to lunch?"

Alzheimer's disease the doctor called it. When Antonio had been a young man, they had simply called it "getting old and losing one's memory." Did naming it make any difference? They still couldn't cure it. And things without names were just as real. A name was just a hook to hang something on. A concept to mull and ponder and worry over even though you didn't understand it and were powerless to change it.

A cream colored sedan pulled into the driveway. Two short taps of the horn and the vigorous wave of the large blond driver greeted them.

"Oh, Christ," Tony muttered. "What's Bill doing here? Doesn't he have some customer to take to lunch and talk over some big land deal with?"

"He likes to eat at home when he can."

Mary stepped to the back door, a woman in her early fifties without a trace of gray in her hair who had thickened to a stout, matronly pouter pigeon. "Papá!" she hollered. "Tony! Bill's here! Lunch!"

"Be nice," Antonio said. "We don't have to argue when we eat. It reminds me too much of when you were kids."

Tony took the old man by the elbow as they walked across the expanse of dried lawn toward the kitchen.

34

It wasn't that Tony disliked his brother-in-law. Bill Pierce was one of those nice, amiable people who smiled a lot. What irritated Tony was that the smiles were sincere. Bill was friendly, naively meeting the world with the innocent expectation that others would like him and treat him fairly. That things would always work out for him. But then Bill was an Anglo, a Texas Anglo, who had always operated from a privileged position. He belonged to a favored group with money and power. Bill just didn't realize it. He thought it was something personal.

"How's it going, Professor?" Bill said.

"There's the Thousand Island dressing over there, or the oil and vinegar. It's too hot for anything other than a salad," Mary said.

"Where are the tortillas?" Antonio asked.

"Oh, Papá. Must you? I have this nice French bread. That's what they eat in California, isn't it, Tony?"

"Croissants," Tony said. "Everything is croissants. Even the fast food places. Croissant sandwiches. Chocolate croissants. There's even a restaurant that advertises New Mexico cooking and serves croissants instead of tortillas."

"You're teasing!"

He grinned and winked at his sister. "I like tortillas," Antonio said. "I've eaten tortillas all of my life. I'm a modern man, but there are some things that are eternal—"

"God. The Church," Tony interrupted.

"—tortillas," Antonio said, frowning at his son.

"What about it, Mary?" Bill asked. His naturally amiable face beamed at her.

She looked around the table from one to the other of them. Then she went to the stove, using a hot pad to pop open the oven and pull out a plate over which she draped a folded dish towel. "One of these days," she said.

"One of these days you're going to forget to take them out, and they'll burn to cinders," Bill said.

"Not while Papá is here."

It was their little game. Mary's way of driving a nail in the coffin of old customs. Papá's way of resisting the rush to the future. Tortillas! Tony thought. What the hell. If it was pita bread, Mary would be forcing it on them. It would be something new and exotic from another culture. Not their culture. Jesus!

"Tony?"

"French bread is fine," he said.

"How's it going, Professor?" Bill repeated. "Any new barricades being stormed these days?"

"Bill!" Mary said sharply.

"There's always the immigration problem," Tony said. His sister shot him a dagger look.

"What I don't understand," Bill said, "is just what a Chicano is. You teach Chicano literature. Now, what's a Chicano?"

"I hate that word!" Mary said. "We're not Chicanos. We're old family Spanish. Descendants of pioneers, of early settlers just like— just like the pilgrims. Only we were here before they were."

"If you've got enough money, you're Spanish," Tony said. "If you're poor, you're Mexican. If you've got the guts to raise your voice and protest, you're Chicano."

Bill's eyebrows rose. He nodded as if he finally understood. "What are they so mad about?" he asked. "I mean, two, three years ago when they picketed that writers' conference in Santa Fe. And before that, during the Bicentennial. They lined the route of the wagon train with their signs. I don't get it."

Tony looked at his father, feeling trapped by Bill's questions. He didn't give a damn what Mary thought. It wouldn't matter what he said anyway. Mary wasn't going to like it. She was too mainstream American to want to remember the past. She would rather turn away from injustice, poverty, the burdens they were fortunate enough not to bear. Let's not talk about such things. Let's pretend that it's all nice. God's in his heaven. The United States really is the land of the free and the home of the brave. She was what some of the more militant referred to as a coconut. Brown on the outside, white on the inside.

"Even in California I saw a photograph of the wagon train," Tony said. "Pioneer costumed gringos in covered wagons led by a police escort. A protestor, his hairy *bigote* framing his smile. Sunglasses shading his eyes. Holding a sign: 'They Came To Remind Us We Are a Conquered People.'

"Being from Texas you should understand conquest. Texas tried to take New Mexico by force twice. In the 1830s and then during the Civil War. Now, finally, they're succeeding. They're migrating to the land of opportunity and buying up all our property."

"Tony! For Christ's sakes!" Mary protested.

Bill shook his head at his wife. "It's all right."

"As for the writers' conference, it was more of the same. One of my colleagues, an Anglo as we say in New Mexico, was there. He was shocked by the protest. They claimed that Kit Carson was a racist."

Mary's face turned a deep red. She turned angrily on Tony. "He married a New Mexican woman. From one of our prominent families. How can you talk such garbage?"

"Children," Antonio said, but his quiet voice was lost in the agitation.

"It wasn't me," Tony said. "It was the protestors. They said that writers about the old West, glorifiers of the cowboy, the John Wayne crowd, had warped history and lied about it. That they villified our Spanish and Indian heritage, making the conquered people the villains in their trashy novels in order to justify their racism and aggression."

Now Bill blushed. "Heavy, heavy," he said. "You mean people really believe that?"

Tony had the good sense to finally shut his mouth. Did he believe what he had just said? Not exactly. The new bigots didn't act that way consciously. They were better rationalizers than their grandparents. They succumbed to hidden assumptions we all make about other people, people different from us, then explained it away. Even Ph.D.s could be bigots these days.

"Please," Antonio said.

"It's better!" Mary protested, looking at her husband and father for confirmation. "Tell him things are better, Papá."

"It's different," Antonio said.

Tony guffawed. "How was it when you were young, Papá?"

The old man's face was not so much pained as serious, wary. "It was different," he said. "Like when your mother and I got married. It was different."

"How different?" Bill asked.

Antonio put a hand on his son-in-law's arm. Tony looked at the bewildered Bill. Here Bill was the outsider, the one who was different. And he was confused. His normally good nature availed him nothing. He was on uncertain ground, unsure of himself. Suddenly the stranger with advantages in the greater society had no special status here. Tony turned away in secret pleasure. His assault had made Bill one of *them*. An outsider. An underdog. But Bill didn't understand that.

"I think—" Antonio began. "I think—it was better."

"Papá!" Mary protested.

"How better?" Bill asked.

"There wasn't all this—this—" The old man waved his hands, grasping for the word.

"Polarization," Tony said.

"Thank you. People weren't at each other's throats. Rights this. Purity of culture that. Young people didn't care if you were Anglo or Spanish American. That's what they started to call us then. Before it had been Mexican. Anyway, they didn't care. We were just people.

"And there weren't so many people, so we got to know each other. We weren't in such a hurry. There was time. We were married in 1928. The year Mickey Mouse was born. The year Shirley Temple was born. The last good year before the Wall Street crash. Oh, it was a good year. It was a peak."

"What changed?" Tony asked.

Antonio squirmed uncomfortably, breaking off a piece of flour tortilla and popping it into his mouth. "The town started to grow. People started to come here from other places."

"Texas!" Tony said.

"Some of them were more—conservative. I guess that's the word. Then there were so many of them that things changed. Not that it's bad. Of course it's not. It's just—different."

Mary stood abruptly, her salad untouched, and stomped from the room.

"Now we've done it," Antonio said.

Tony looked across the table at his brother-in-law. "I didn't mean to start this, Bill. We're just talking. Just good old-fashioned college dormitory bullshit. It's not personal. God, it's not personal. Mary!" he shouted. "I'm sorry!"

"You do have a way with words," Bill said.

Tony stood, bumping the edge of the table and spilling iced tea. "Mary!" He hurried to the living room. She was seated on the sofa, her hands in her lap, glaring angrily at the floor.

"I'm sorry, Mary. We were just talking. I didn't mean anything."

"What about my children?" Mary said, her mouth twisted in anguish. "What about my children?"

"They're fine. Bill's a good lawyer and Susie's a rising journalist."

"That's not what I mean. Why should they be at war with themselves just because their parents came from two different groups? What difference does that make?"

"None at all. That's the point."

"You have a hell of a way of saying it. Why do you have to come here and criticize everything anyway? You're not even a New Mexican anymore. You're a Californian."

"Maybe that's why it's easier to criticize," he said. He was sorry, truly sorry. Usually their arguments were playful, more teasing than real. But somehow, as you made your way in the world, things got complicated and confusing. Good God, what was wrong with siring half-breeds? Wasn't that what the melting pot was all about?

"Please, Mary. Don't stay angry at me. You know how I am."

"Yes, damn it!" But when he took her hand, she squeezed it back. "You're just angry because they didn't want to do your play," she said. "That's it, isn't it?"

He winced. The truth hurt. Especially when you ran into it head on and unexpectedly.

"That's it, isn't it?" Oh, she was a sly one.

"No," he said. "I was just talking."

"Then you'd better apologize to Bill."

"I did."

She rose and went to the bathroom to rinse her face. Tony sat a moment, wondering what it was that drove him sometimes. Why wasn't he warm like Mary? Or easygoing, indifferent really, like their oldest sister, Stella? Or more pliable, a Hispanic version of Bill, like his older brother, Joe? Why was he the one of all of them who faced the world with his chin thrust forward, his fists doubled, and his tongue too ready to challenge?

He walked thoughtfully back to the kitchen. Antonio and Bill stopped talking. Had they been talking about him? His ears should have been burning.

After an awkward silence, Antonio said, "Thank you, Bill. But really, you don't have to be there. Mary and Tony are going with me."

There are already too many real estate developers on that committee, Tony thought. And lawyers. When they get around to appointing a poet, then maybe they can add another land developer.

"No hard feelings," Tony said to Bill.

Bill stood, slapped him on the shoulder, then hurried to look for Mary before returning to the office.

35

There were no signs on the doors, so Antonio asked a dark young woman behind the city hall information desk. She pointed down the hall to the left. They were early. Tony was always early when he drove. The three of them took chairs around the large walnut table and waited. There were eight members on the committee who would soon arrive. Plus representatives from the city government, including someone from the Parks Department.

"This is your last chance, Papá," Mary said.

"It's only money," Tony said in disgust.

"Quite a lot of money. Bill says—"

"Please," Antonio said. "No arguments. Your mother wants to give it to the city."

"But it seems such a waste," Mary said.

"We've been all through this before. This is the way it's going to be!"

Tony could hear Bill's slight drawl, not really too much of Texas left there, as he explained to Antonio all the reasons why he should sell the property. He would sum it up with a rousing tribute to free enterprise, competition, and enlightened self-interest, not understanding what it was that might cause someone to want to give. Give was not in his everyday vocabulary. It had been replaced by negotiate, backscratch, fair market value, deal.

"Papá is so stubborn," Mary whispered to Tony.

The door opened cautiously. "Hello, folks." It was the committee chairman. Another of those endless variations of his brother-in-law with a more pronounced drawl, a redder sunburnt complexion, and a slightly country manner. A diamond in the rough making his way in the big city.

The rest of the committee straggled in, some nodding at their guests whom most had never met. It was what Tony expected: six men and two women. Only two were Hispanic. The Anglos for the most part speaking in that Southwestern drawl that could have been Texas, Oklahoma, Arizona, or New Mexico. It was the sort of countrified accent that irritated him the way that the soft Spanish accent of many of his own people irritated some of these Anglos.

After a few minutes of chitchat, the latecomers rushed in: the man from the Parks Department, a representative from the mayor's office, members of the city council—a mirror image of the committee.

The chairman stood and smiled with the awkward uncertainty of one who wants to please. "If the meeting will come to order," he drawled. "As you know, one of the items on the agenda is, uh, the park that one of the pioneer families of this historic city is donating as part of the centennial. With us today is one of our, uh, distinguished citizens, Mr. Antonio Rafa. Mr. Rafa's wife, a member of the prominent Armijo family, is unable to join us, but other members of the, uh, family are here. Because of this important and unusual item, I suggest that we, uh, dispense with the minutes of the last meeting."

All eyes turned on them. Some smiled. Antonio nodded in acknowledgment, while the Parks Department representative squirmed uncomfortably in his chair, his face strained with concern.

The chairman read from a document on the table. His head was turned down, his chin against his thick neck, the drawl more than normally halting. Everybody already knew what he read. He droned on anyway, like a priest determined to preach his sermon in spite of hooded eyes, disguised yawns, and a snore or two.

"So you see," he concluded. "That's where the, uh, matter stands as of now. It only needs agreement from this group for the legal steps to be taken. I urge that we, uh, resolve it today because the date of the centennial celebration is galloping right at us.

"Mr. Rafa," he said, his voice rising as if to punctuate the name with a question mark.

"Your honor," Antonio said in a nervous flurry. "Members of the committee. We're ready. My son-in-law is in real estate and my grandson is a lawyer. They're ready to meet with your people so we can sign the land over to the city. We've been ready for weeks."

One of the city council members looked with raised eyebrows at the chairman. "What's the delay?"

There was a buzz of embarrassed conversation. Then the man from the Parks Department leaned over the table with intense and aggressive agitation. Tony, meanwhile, looked at his father in surprise.

Hadn't this all been settled? The celebration was to start in a few days. What the hell had they been doing all these months?

"Just a little red tape," Antonio whispered to him. "I'm ready to sign it over to them today."

"Mr. Chairman." The man from the Parks Department looked as if he were ready to leap across the table. "Mr. Chairman! We haven't resolved the question of the park name. Until we do that—"

"Jesus Christ!" Tony muttered.

The man from the mayor's office glared across the table. "Is that what's holding this up? A name?" he asked incredulously.

The group erupted into noisy conversation, much of it aimed at the Parks Department. "Ladies and gentlemen. Please," the chairman pleaded. He searched desperately for the gavel. He finally found it on the floor behind an easel holding a pad of blank paper. Three raps on the table brought the group to silence.

"Ladies and gentlemen," he said. "We've got to resolve this. The celebration starts day after tomorrow. We won't even, uh, have time to get, uh, plaques engraved. And we haven't decided what music to play as, uh, part of the dedication."

"Granada," one of the committee members said.

"Forget it!" a Hispanic on the city council barked.

"Jesus Christ!" Tony muttered, looking with alarm first at his father and then at his sister. This was worse than a meeting of the college faculty.

"Ladies and gentlemen. Ladies and gentlemen." The chairman rapped on the table again. "Let's talk about the name. Now, George, uh, just what the hell—pardon my French—is all this about a name?"

Now that he was the center of attention, the man from the Parks Department relaxed and cleared his throat. He looked around importantly, preening himself.

"We have a new policy on naming parks," he said. "It was approved by the mayor and the city council. As you all know, we have over one hundred parks in this city. Sometimes they're named for the street on which they're located. Sometimes for the particular part of town they're in, like Los Duranes Park. Or in commemoration of historic events like Bataan Park. Or for people, like Pat Hurley Park and Pete Padilla Park.

"The responsibility and final decision for naming new parks rests solely with the Parks Department. The policy is to alternate names in sequence as I've already mentioned: streets, parts of town, historic events, and people. It just so happens that it's the turn of a historic event to be used to name a park. For example, Centennial Park."

One of the city councilmen who had been glowering throughout the explanation spoke up. "Look," he said. "The council approved acceptance of this gift over three months ago. As far as we're concerned, the park is ready to go. Now why has it taken three months? I'm stunned, absolutely stunned, that the ownership of the land hasn't been transferred yet. The donor is obviously willing. All because of some new procedure on park names. This is unbelievable!"

A woman interrupted. "Centennial Park may be all right. I have no objection myself. Except that of the over one hundred city parks, only thirty have Spanish names. I think that's terrible and needs to be changed. The land being donated is in Los Rafas, one of the historic settlements in the city. I mean, we have Los Duranes Park and Barelas Community Center, and Martíneztown Park. Every old Spanish hamlet seems to have a park except Los Rafas. Why can't it be called Los Rafas Park?"

Well, Tony thought, this is going to take longer than anyone thought. And it did, with members alternately berating the Parks Department for negligence and arguing over what the park ought to be named. When Antonio repeatedly raised his hand, he was ignored. His too polite protests were swept away like a piece of tissue in a high desert wind. Mary shook her head in disbelief, patting her father's arm and whispering that everything would work out all right by the grace of God.

Finally, exasperated and red-faced, the chairman banged the gavel repeatedly. "God damn it! Uh, let's get this wagon out of the mud and on the trail." The committee members exchanged knowing glances. "First of all, we need to take the legal steps for the, uh, property to be turned over to the city."

Antonio nodded. "That's what I've been trying to say. I'm ready anytime. Today. Now. I just have to call my son-in-law and grandson. But—"

"Right!" the chairman said. "The site has already been, uh, surveyed and cleared for a dedication. We can use a blank plaque that can be engraved and installed later. As for the, uh, name—" He looked around the table cautiously. "How would, uh, Centennial Park do?"

"The Parks Department—" their representative began.

But Antonio was shaking his head, even as the chairman turned toward him. "No!" the old man said.

"No?"

The uproar began again.

"Nobody even asked him about the name," Mary said.

"It's Mamá's land," Tony said. "It still is."

There was a deathly silence. A pained recognition lit the eyes of the chairman. "What's that?" he stammered.

"Nobody even asked him," Tony said.

The silence was overwhelming. Even the sound of their breathing faded as if life had been suspended. Sixteen pairs of eyes turned on the three of them: the indignant Antonio, the equally indignant Mary, and Tony, whose anger writhed restlessly in the firm but weakening grip of his better judgment.

"Didn't anyone read the letter I sent to the city council?" Antonio asked. The council members looked at each other in embarrassment, and then at the Parks Department member accusingly. "The park is to be named for my wife. Actually it's her land, passed on from her father. It is to be named Leonor Park."

A low buzz of consternation rose from the group. "But it's a Parks Department policy—" their representative began.

Fuck your policy! Tony almost shouted. But he choked back his anger as Mary spoke out. "Leonor Park!" she said. "That or nothing!"

The chairman looked around the table as if trying to escape. "It has to be dedicated this week," he insisted. "We already gave the, uh, story to the newspapers." As if that conferred a reality that thereby became irrevocable. He faced the man from the Parks Department, his small, red eyes gleaming in outrage. "Pardon my French, but, uh, what the hell has the Parks Department been doing this past three months? No wonder the trees around town are dying. The mayor is going to hear about this!"

One of the city councilmen turned to the chairman. "I remember the letter. Señor Rafa is right. It said that it was supposed to be named Leonor Park."

Then the woman who had championed Los Rafas Park nodded emphatically. "Leonor Rafa Park," she said. "Another Spanish name."

Antonio shook his head. "Leonor Park," he repeated. "Leonor Park. Or nothing."

36

Leonor Park was dedicated on Sunday, July 7, at one-thirty in the afternoon. It was a still, bright, hot day. The sky was the clear blue of the high desert that lets you see an object miles away as if it were next to you. The light was of that compelling clarity that made artists euphoric. That unhinged the skulls of philosophers so that the sun burned directly into their brains. That expanded the minds of the religious and mystical from their earthly focus to the ultimate contemplation of the infinite. It was a disturbing clarity of sky that brooked no self-deception. That told the discernng that all was one: man, sky, earth, God Himself.

The small gathering stood in their Sunday best in the shade of a grove of cottonwood trees, languid in the summer heat. Antonio and Leonor Rafa were in a semicircle with the committee chairman, a city council representative, and the head of the Parks Department, waiting for the mayor. Facing them was the rest of the family: Tony, Mary and Bill Pierce, the Pierces' son and wife with small daughter, and the Pierces' unmarried daughter. Tony's elder sister, Stella, and his elder brother, Joe, had driven in for the day. Stella from Santa Fe with husband, and Joe from Truth or Consequences sans wife.

Antonio stood with his hand resting on the back of Leonor's wheelchair. She had been dressed formally and neatly by her nurse. Her eyes were closed in repose. Beside her stood the pastor of San Felipe Church who, in keeping with the changing times, was to be a spectator rather than a participant.

There was a stir from the roadside. A young woman rushed exitedly, camera ready, as the faint wail of a siren grew louder. Two cars braked to a stop. The police disembarked first, leading the mayor and his entourage through the gate in the barbed wire fence.

Then the reporters and photographers came rushing up, following the mayor who smiled and nodded as cameras flashed. The chairman stepped forward and whispered urgently as the camera crew focused on the ceremonial gathering. Out of camera range under the staunch, upright trees stood the family and a few spectators.

"All right?" the mayor said to the television cameraman and the young woman who held the microphone. "Are we on?"

His smile flashed as if the whirring camera had switched it on. The words were brief, a tribute to this celebration and a remembrance of the city's beginnings. With the gracious acceptance of a gift from one of the city's pioneer families.

It was not a ceremony to remember. Perhaps ten seconds on the six o'clock news, Tony thought, then oblivion. How different from that first ceremony of taking possession of this land "once, twice, and thrice, and all the times I can and must, of the actual jurisdiction, civil as well as—" Those words of the early Spanish settler of New Mexico, Don Juan de Oñate, husband of a great-granddaughter of Emperor Moctezuma of Mexico. The historic Spanish ceremony where the leader reached down to earth, took a handful of dirt and grass, and tossed it into the sky. The breeze scattered it east, west, north, south "in the name of the most holy Trinity, and of the eternal Unity, Deity, and Majesty, God the Father, the Son, and the Holy Ghost."

Yes, how different. With the priest as a spectator, not a participant. With his brother-in-law, Bill, watching ruefully as a realtor's commission died stillborn with the land given rather than sold. With his mother, eyes open now, holding his father's hand. The givers knowing that the Great Giver would come and take them away, sooner rather than later.

"—and so, in the name of this fair city, we dedicate this as Leonor Park, for the welfare and pleasure of our citizens." The mayor was finished.

The chairman handed him the plaque. Flashbulbs blazed as they posed with it chest high. Then the head of the Parks Department brought two new shovels, handing one each to the mayor and chairman. They stepped aside, exposing to view the two small flowering trees in cans, one for each of Leonor's surnames, the Armijo to which she was born, and the Rafa which she married.

More flashbulbs blazed. Then the mayor and chairman passed the shovels to Antonio and Leonor. The old man dug deep into the hole that was ready for a tree. It was a firm, healthy thrust. Then he took his wife's shovel, placed a portion of dry dirt on it, and with his hands over hers, tossed it beside the nearer of the two holes.

There were cheers and polite applause. The mayor shook hands all around. Then he rushed across the field to the police car with top light still circling.

"Thank you," the chairman said. "Thank you very much."

The ceremony was over. The small group dispersed. Tony followed Mary and Bill across the shade to their parents.

"That was lovely," Leonor said. "Now I can die in peace."

"Now, now," Antonio said, patting her shoulder.

Mother was alert and alive, almost normal, Tony thought. He leaned over and kissed her cheek. "Yes," she said, nodding at Tony. "Grandpa Armijo cheated some poor farmer out of this land in the first place. Then my Aunt Magdalena used it to drive some poor tenant farmer to starvation. They took so much from others, Grandpa and Auntie. Then Papá, poor Papá. He had been poor so long he had forgotten how to spend it, so he left it all to me. Some of it, a little of it, ought to be given back."

Bill cradled his granddaughter who had leaned her head on his shoulder, nodding off. His eyes flickered with the dying glow of chances lost as he surveyed the tract that had been newly leveled, ready for landscaping.

"You know," Leonor said. "They should have named it for the people who owned it first. For the Rafas."

Or better yet, Tony thought. For the Pueblo Indians who lived here before the first white man. Or for their unnamed ancestors, the New World twins of Adam and Eve. Didn't the early European settlers claim that this place, this desert, was the twin of that other Holy Land?

"No," Antonio said. "It's named for you."

Tony was surprised by the emotion in his father's voice. Then he realized that though named Leonor Park, it had not been named just for her. That it was named as much for his father, for that tangible memory he would keep to his dying day. For Antonio knew that Leonor would go first, and he could not bear it.

The rest of the family gathered around. "I'm hungry," Joe said. "When do we eat?"

"Will you join us, Father?" Antonio asked the priest.

Tony stepped behind the wheelchair and started across the field toward the open, crude gate.

"I reserved a private room at Las Casitas," Antonio said to the priest. "You know how full of tourists Old Town is on Sunday. You have to wait forever."

Tony lifted his mother into the back seat of the car, folded the wheelchair, and packed it in the trunk. His father sat beside her. It was a short drive, past the museum and into Old Town plaza. If it had not been for Leonor and for the heat, they could have walked it easily.

"You never finished your story," Tony said, looking up into the rearview mirror at his father.

* * *

No one knew why Magdalena had driven south to the Barelas Bridge when Corrales was north and the Old Town Bridge was so much closer. The Barelas Bridge was still under construction and would not be finished until that fall. Perhaps she had driven past Nicolás's house looking for the young people. Perhaps she had been confused, suffering the aftereffects of her heavy drinking.

Whatever the reason, when the first work crew drove their truck to the bridge site early the next morning, Joe Padilla looked out of the driver's window and saw a huge black Packard sedan like an over-turned turtle, lying half submerged in the water, wedged against a sandbar.

First the police came, approaching as close as they safely could—the river was at a dangerous level because of recent heavy rains—and were only able to see a dark shape. The ambulance and tow truck arrived soon after. It was then that they found the middle-aged woman dressed in black, an ugly gash across her forehead, the wind-shield a spider's web of cracked glass. She hung upside down, a look of startled anger on her face as if being found that way was the ultimate affront. The local newspaper headline read: "Proprietress of Speak-easy Drowns. Suicide Suspected Because of Legal Difficulties."

* * *

"There is justice after all," Tony said.

"Well, maybe."

The response surprised Tony. He wondered if the old man had really heard him. But the thoughtful expression on Antonio's face told him otherwise.

"The mills of the gods grind slow. Time wounds all heels. What you sow you shall reap. How many clichés are there?" Tony said.

Antonio's solemn lack of response made Tony uncomfortable. He felt a childlike panic, a throwback to his boyhood, at his father's silent judgment. He felt the need to talk and explain. To change his father's mind even though he did not know what his father's mind was.

"The good guys are supposed to win," Tony said, his speech accelerating so that each word seemed to trip on the heels of the word before. "Isn't that what justice is all about?"

"If inanimate things could only talk," Antonio said.

Yes, Tony thought. The earth would open and its voice would thunder disapproval at us.

"All you have to do," Antonio said, "is look around this plaza and think of who stole what from whom, not just in our lifetime, but all the way back to the beginning."

"Yes. And like I said, there is justice after all. The right side finally won one. Greed gets its comeuppance. It's nothing grand like conquering a continent, winning a war, or taming a wilderness. People aren't giants anymore. Our passions have been civilized down to the level of soap opera. And right wins one of its rare battles against might."

"It wasn't greed," Antonio said. "That's too simple. It was fear."

Tony was startled. Fear? Now he knew that the old man had strayed into some bizarre fairyland.

"Magdalena reached out to grab because she hoped that having enough would protect her. It was her lack of faith. Her belief that the world was running out of—of everything. That if she did not grab, and grab enough to last a lifetime, she would be lost. Her goal was survival. She was no different than the rest of us."

"Oh, come on, Papá. I'm shocked. You mean after all the dirty things she did you feel sorry for her? I don't believe that."

"You think that if the right people get killed everything will come out all right? Is that what you think?"

"Sure."

"Then tell me, who are the right people?" Tony's mouth dropped open. Wasn't it obvious? Arguing with his father was like arguing with his wife.

"Remember," Antonio continued, "when you telephoned from California the day President Kennedy was assassinated? How the John

Birch professor whose office was next to yours came running over, his eyes wild with excitement? 'They got the son-of-a-bitch!' he said. 'Now if they just get a few more in Washington everything will be all right.' Remember? If you hadn't telephoned me and cooled off, you'd have attacked the man."

Tony remembered. But he didn't see what his father was driving at. "Don't you see that this is the same thing?" Antonio asked. Tony shook his head. "If all we have to do is kill the right person it would be simple. But who decides who the right person is? And if someone doesn't agree that it's the right person, that someone will seek revenge. It's the way things have always been."

"Oh, Papá. Jesus. This isn't the end of the world. Just some greedy old witch committing suicide because she lost some money. Nothing grand. No empires lost. Just another soap opera. Would the world have been better off if she had lived? Would Mother have been better off? It's just one of those lucky things."

"Well, let me tell you about another of those lucky things. I haven't finished the story yet."

Tony was in no mood to listen. He didn't like arguing with his father. This sweet, gentle old man who had turned into some kind of moral philosopher in his old age. What was the world coming to? But Antonio told him anyway.

It wasn't cowboys and Indians, Antonio said. The white hats against the black hats. Good against evil. It was the human condition, where we all fought with our own weapons for our own reasons.

One must not be deceived by one's heart any more than by one's mind. Just because Nicolás was a gentle, ineffectual soul did not make him a saint—or anything near it. Who was it that telephoned that fearful and superstitious woman disguising his voice and claiming to be her father back from the grave? It was Nicolás.

For that matter, who reported Magdalena to the revenuers? No one ever found out. It could have been almost anyone. One of her ex-husbands. One of her tenants or ex-tenants. It might even have been Nicolás. Some suspected him. And Nicolás always avoided the subject, as if it was more than he wanted to consider.

Just because Nicolás gave most of what he inherited to Leonor did not absolve him. Stealing to give to someone who may even deserve it does not make stealing right. Whether you call it Manifest Destiny or protecting your darling daughter. It was conscience money. Trying to make up for all those years of neglect. Like Magdalena said: he had no guts. He wanted to slide off the problems in his life. Be bailed out by his father's money. Let someone else take over his responsibilities to his daughter. While he wrung his hands and played the poor survivor after his wife's death. He didn't even have the courage to marry again.

Only later in life did Leonor finally see this. She was only eighteen when her aunt died. What did she know? But she saw after Nicolás came to live with us. In just a few years he was suddenly an old man. We didn't know why. Except that not long after his sister's death he became ill. Soon he sold his share of the Wigwam Motor Court because he could no longer carry out his part of the work. He would sit in a rocking chair, just like his father, with a Navajo blanket over his shoulders and doze off if he didn't want to hear what you were saying to him.

It was after this that his part of the story came out. His telephone calls to Magdalena that seemed to haunt him as much as they had haunted her. About how the world would be a better place if people would just be nice to each other. About the fortunes he could have made: in colored sheep or the movies or radio. Yet in back of it all, regrets. Deep regrets that seemed to be the virus that caused his last disease.

So, poor man. A gentle soul. But was he any less to blame than Magdalena? Probably not. The only difference was that he knew it, while she never would have. So he only spent what little he needed from his father's estate. When he really started to decline, with something the doctors could finally diagnose, what his father had left was almost intact. "It's yours," he said to Leonor. "You deserve it."

When Leonor finally understood what had happened, that guilt had hastened her father's death, she tried to forget what Nicolás had left her. It was tainted money, tainted land. She knew too much of its history. When she became ill, she realized that her illness was a warning. She was the inheritor of takers and had to earn whatever forgiveness she could by giving something back. So there it was. The park. A penance you might say. An offer in atonement if only God would accept it. It was right that it should be for everyone to enjoy, which is what it was in the beginning anyway.

*   *   *

"One last thing," Tony said. "Was it suicide? Did Magdalena finally despair of the things she had done?"

"She would never have killed herself. She was too selfish. It was a foolish accident like so many things in life."

When they pulled in behind the restaurant, Joe rushed from the other car for his turn at the wheelchair. Tony lagged behind with his father. Just before they entered Las Casitas, Antonio stopped and pointed toward the parking lot. "See that building?"

Tony glanced down the narrow alley. "The bookstore?"

"That used to be your great-aunt's café."

"The speakeasy?"

Antonio nodded. Everything changes, Tony thought. A speakeasy then, a bookstore and souvenir shop now. And this old plaza, he thought, taking one last look across the square toward San Felipe Church. Once the center of town, the center of a settlement, the center of another way of life. Now just another quaint tourist trap.